The Cowboy's Choice

THE GOVAIN COWBOYS, Volume 2

Janalyn Knight

Published by Janalyn Knight, 2019.

To Patty, my loyal friend of many years. You've gotten me through life's awful storms and I love you.

Chapter One

LARA COLE'S HAND TREMBLED. As she slid the back off the stem of her earring, it fell on the floor. If this is what happened when she thought of Adam Govain, how could she handle meeting him face to face?

His mother, Millie, had contacted Lara's mom and asked if Adam and Caleb could have the honor of being pall bearers for Lara's father, Emmett, who died suddenly four days ago of a brain aneurysm. Her father had been the Govain family attorney for many years, and aside from serving them in his professional capacity, he had been their friend.

Lara found the small silver back and put her earring on, then tied a scarf over her head, covering her long curls. The wind blew fiercely outside, and a thunderstorm threatened any minute. Grabbing two umbrellas in case her mother didn't have one, she stepped out into the maelstrom of whirling fall leaves and made her way to her car. The early September day should have been warm, but the bite in the air chilled her. As she opened her door, a gust tore it from her grasp. Grabbing the handle with both hands, she pulled the door toward her until she could sit in her seat, closing it with a loud click.

Shaken and shivering, she sat for a minute. This was a terrible day to say goodbye to her dad, and she had no idea how her mom would face the funeral with the sure-to-be wet and turbulent weather at the cemetery service.

Losing her husband had devastated Jenna Cole. Emmitt had handled everything in their lives. She never made major decisions or managed the finances. She would be lost without him. Lara would need to step in and provide comfort and support in many areas.

Thirty minutes later, Lara entered the already filled-to-capacity church, her arm around her mother. Lara glanced around the gathering, looking for familiar faces, and from the second pew, Adam Govain's gaze smacked into hers. Eyes wide, she froze. Her heart thudded, and her pulse raced so fast she was immediately light headed.

He nodded and the corner of his mouth quirked up.

With a tight nod in return, she led her mother to the first pew and took her seat.

Unwelcome thoughts of Adam invaded her mind. His dark hair was the same, as was his tall, broad-shouldered frame. Why did his smile still melt her insides after thirteen long years?

A baby made a fussy noise, and she glanced back to see a tiny girl trying to get down from Caleb's lap.

Adam brandished his mirrored sunglasses before the child, and she quieted. Taking the girl in his arms, he bounced her up and down as she put his glasses in her mouth.

Seeing Adam cuddling the baby sent shockwaves through Lara. Was he married? Was that his child? Oh God, she needed out of this place! Whipping her head back around, she bit down on her lip hard enough for the pain to take her mind off of who sat behind her. Her focus today must be her mother—helping her find the strength to make it through the services without falling apart.

The pastor stepped up to the lectern and began to speak.

ADAM CUDDLED HIS LITTLE niece, Abi, distracting himself from the vision of the older, and even more beautiful, Lara who had just walked down the aisle. Her face had lost the rounded teen-aged look of the past and now showed striking cheekbones, a classic jawline and sensuous lips. Her long slender throat led to the full breasts he remembered so well.

Abi dove for the floor again, squawking loudly, and Eve reached across Caleb's lap.

Adam absent mindedly handed the baby to his sister-in-law looking at the fall of glorious dark curls in front of him, wishing he could see those clear grey eyes again that had captured him as Lara entered the church. Damn, she was gorgeous, with her hair curling nearly to her waist. She was slender now—almost too thin—just so different from the shapely, happy teenager he'd loved and left behind.

His stomach clenched. What had she felt when their gazes met? Did her heart leap as his had? Were thoughts of the two of them swirling in her head as they were in his? Or did she forget all about what they had shared? It was a lifetime ago, but now that she was home again, it seemed like yesterday.

As the pastor spoke, Adam relived memories of high school and Lara: Family dinners, dark movie theaters and stolen kisses, riding horses on his ranch, and senior prom. God, she was hot in that dress. Deep red with a low cut back, her breasts showing just enough to tantalize him—he'd wanted every guy on the dancefloor to see her and know she was his.

Afterward, he parked with her out in one of the big pastures and laid a blanket in the back of his truck. Closing his eyes, he could still remember the excitement when he took the dress off Lara and made love to her, naked, with only the moon as witness.

She gave her all to him—never held back. He knew how much she loved him. That was why, when she begged him for the last time to change his mind and go with her to California for college, he knew he broke her heart. He turned his back on their love, on Lara, to make his dream of becoming a top trauma surgeon come true.

He and Lara didn't speak again after they parted. Though he called, she had asked her parents not to give him her number at school. Shit, that hurt. He realized then that she wanted him out of her life. It had taken years to forget her.

Caleb rose. Adam had daydreamed through the entire funeral. Hoping to catch Lara's eyes, he kept his gaze glued to her. She never looked his way as she helped her mother stand and escorted her past the pews toward the back of the church.

The two women seemed so fragile—so vulnerable. Adam had to restrain himself from rushing to Lara's side, throwing his arm around her shoulders, and lending her his strength. Why was she alone? Had she never married? Did she have children? He needed to know everything about her now that he'd finally seen her again. Joining the throng of people leaving their seats, he made his way to his truck.

Thirty minutes later, Adam drove into the cemetery where trees thrashed and rain had started to pelt the blacktop. Quite a few people had already arrived. Black umbrellas blew crazily in the wind and coats unworn for months whipped open exposing their owners to the wrath of the oncoming storm.

He got out and leaned into the wind, forging his way to the lines of chairs at the gravesite. Caleb had saved him a seat beside him. Lara and her mother were seated in the front row—Lara with her arm around her mother's shoulders. Moving to his seat, Adam's gaze was drawn to Lara's hair as it waved behind her like a flag. Adam couldn't take his eyes off of her.

Just then the hearse arrived. Caleb nudged him, and they headed that way as wayward leaves from the oaks overhead blew this way and that in the air. The attendant rolled the casket out, and Adam and Caleb took the first two handles. Other friends stepped up and slipped their hands through the remaining grips. Rain came down harder now. It was difficult to keep his eyes clear. Caleb started them out. They pressed forward into the wind, making their way to the burial site and placing Lara's father on the lowering device set across the grave.

Adam stood and turned toward the crowd of mourners, ready to return to his seat, and stopped. As soon as he saw Lara, she saw him, and her eyes widened. He tried to hold her gaze but she whipped her head to the side.

Dammit. Now that she was in town, she was all he could think about. He wanted to talk to her—wanted to know all about her life. In fact, it was more than want, he *needed* to know these things.

As he sat next to his brother, he grabbed his umbrella and opened it. In a whisper loud enough to be heard over the storm, he asked, "Is Lara Cole married?"

Caleb, under his own umbrella, shrugged. "I don't know. I haven't heard anything about her."

The pastor, promising to keep his words short, began the service but Adam tuned him out. Having Lara so close drove everything else from his mind. She looked pale, didn't she? Was she sick? He didn't remember her being so fair. Of course, they spent a lot of time in the sun back in high school. Maybe she didn't get outside much anymore. What was her life like now? What was *she* like?

Caleb and Eve stood, rain streaming from their umbrellas, and Adam realized the graveside service was over. He had a vague recollection that he made some response, but he couldn't recall any of it. He followed his brother away from the uncomfortable metal chairs.

A few people walked over to Lara and her mother, but most ran for their cars.

When Adam started in Lara's direction, Caleb caught his arm. "There's a reception at their house. Let them get in out of this downpour, and speak to them there, brother."

Adam nodded and jogged toward his truck.

Vehicles were lined up and down the residential street where Lara's mother lived and were even parked on the next street over. Adam gave up trying to find a parking spot, ending up a block away. Walking in the rain meant his pant legs were soaked by the time he arrived at the house that had been a part of his high school years. It hadn't really changed much since then. He stepped up on the porch and shook his umbrella, then went through the front door that had been left open to welcome guests. The house was packed with bodies, most with plates in their hands, and his eyes searched for Lara among them.

Her mother, Jenna, sat on the couch with friends sitting beside her, a plate of untouched food on her lap. She appeared dazed and frail, and his heart went out to her. Changing direction, he went over and knelt in front of her, taking her hand. "I'm so sorry for your loss. Emmett was a wonderful man and a good friend to us. If you need anything, I'm here for you." He pulled two cards from his wallet and wrote his cell number on the back of them, handing one to her. "I mean it. Call me if I can help." He held her hand again.

She smiled and gripped his fingers. "Adam, you were always a good boy, and now you're a sweet man, just like your daddy. Thank you, honey."

He spied Lara as she entered the room, and with a smile, stood and headed toward her. Before he reached her, however, a woman snagged Lara's attention and drew her away. Still soaking wet, he went to find the coffee.

When he came back into the living room, he spotted Lara saying goodbye to a guest and walked over to stand behind her.

With a last farewell, she turned around. Stepping back quickly, her mouth ajar, she said, "Adam, you startled me."

"Lara, I need to talk to you." Damn, he'd just blurted that out. "I mean, I'd love to catch up with you—find out how you are."

She took another step back. "I'm fine." Squaring her shoulders, she said, "I have to take care of my guests and help my mother get through today. I can't."

He let out the breath he was holding. Shit. Was she still mad at him after all these years? He was a good guy back then and had treated her right. He just couldn't, *wouldn't*, give up the college opportunity he dreamed of. He'd trained under and worked with some of the best trauma doctors in the country at Boston Medical, and the facility was state of the art. His career couldn't have had a better start.

But she was right. Today, this setting, wasn't the time to talk to her. "I understand. And, Lara? I'm so sorry about your dad. He was a great guy. I'm here for you if you need me." Pressing his card into her hand, he walked out the open door.

On his way home, his phone rang. "Adam Govain."

A voice he recognized said, "How's it going?"

He smiled. "Gerry, what's up, man?" Gerry was a friend from college who ended up moving to Texas and working in Dallas. They'd stayed in touch through the years.

Gerry said, "I'm wondering if you ever followed through on that job I told you about. Opportunities at a Level I Trauma Center don't come along very often. Especially where one of their leadership team is old as dirt and you'd have a leg up on the position when it comes available."

"Yeah, I sent my CV in a couple of weeks ago." He'd met every challenge at Ft. Stockton's small hospital with ease. It would be nice to work in a fast-paced, stimulating trauma environment again.

"Awesome. It would be cool to have you close, bro'. Keep me posted if you hear anything, okay?" Gerry said.

"I will."

Back at home, he kicked his shoes off at the door and laid on the couch. Arms behind his head, his thoughts returned to Lara. He had to talk with her. There must be a way to break through the barrier she held between them. He wouldn't give up on her now that he'd found her again.

Chapter Two

LARA SHIVERED IN DREAD as she unzipped the back of her dress in her bedroom. She'd worked at her father's office for a few hours today, and even that short time had exhausted her. She gave her notice at her firm in San Diego when her mother called with the news of her dad's death. His dream was always that Lara would take over his practice when he retired. His passing made that decision for her. Her mother couldn't live without money from the business each month. Lara had already hired a moving company and would fly back in a couple of days to pack her personal things and bring back more clothes.

Life didn't seem real right now. It was like a bad dream where she'd wake and everything would go back to normal. Her mom was suffering so badly. She and Lara's father had been high school sweethearts and had still enjoyed such a happy marriage. Lara always thought of them as the perfect couple. So far, her mother wasn't coping with her husband's death well at all. She wouldn't eat and only slept when Lara made her take a sleeping pill. The rest of the time she paced the floors in their home, telling her daughter that she felt her husband's presence—that she didn't think he'd passed on to heaven.

Lara finished undressing and threw on a robe. Her father's assistant would be a great help to Lara while she got up to speed on her dad's open cases. Nothing critical was due in court in the next week, so she had time to go home to San Diego, get some things packed and return to Ft. Stockton before she stepped into the traces full time.

As she reached for the light switch, her gaze landed on her dresser top and the business card she'd tossed there yesterday afternoon. A rush of anxiety swept through her. She couldn't face the complications Adam brought to her life, not with everything else ahead of her. Losing her father, the man who'd taught her that she was smart and tough and could be anything she wanted to in life, was a devastating blow. She didn't have the luxury of giving into her pain. Not with the mess her mother was. To make it through the next few months, Lara would have to keep a tight rein on her emotions, focus hard on learning her father's client load, and find ways to help her mother cope with her loss.

That left no room for Adam Govain and the whole shitload of pain that man brought with him.

He knew nothing of her tragedy. She'd wanted it that way. She said goodbye to him the day before she left for college in San Diego. Two weeks into her life at her freshman dorm, she missed her first period. Then she missed another. A trip to the campus clinic confirmed her fears. She was pregnant. Adam had always used a condom. They were careful. But something obviously went wrong. There was no question in her mind about telling him. He made his decision to leave her, and she wasn't about to drag him back with the news of an unplanned pregnancy.

At her dorm, she locked the door and cried for hours. Should she terminate? Should she raise the baby on her own and quit school when it came time to give birth? Maybe she should have the baby and give it up for adoption. Could she do that after carrying her child in her body for a whole nine months? No matter what happened, she was determined that her parents wouldn't know about her pregnancy. This was her problem, and she'd handle it on her own.

Two weeks later, she decided to keep her baby and put the child up for adoption at birth. The campus clinic gave her some agency referrals, and she made several calls, set up interviews, and eventually settled on one, signing the paperwork soon after.

Despite knowing that others would raise her baby, she came to love it. As her belly grew, so did her joy. When she first experienced the tiny butterfly movements of her daughter, she cried with happiness.

Four and a half months into her pregnancy, the unthinkable happened—she started to spot, then to bleed, accompanied by excruciating cramps. Before her doctor arrived to meet her at the ER, Lara aborted, passing the placenta and fetal tissue. Light headed and in shock, she stared at the greyish mass and blood clots between her legs, horrified that she'd lost her precious baby.

She knew that somehow it was her fault. She didn't love her baby enough or she should have taken better care of herself. Inconsolable, and having told no one in her family about her pregnancy, she had nobody to turn to in her grief.

Spiraling out of control, she drank heavily, let her grades slip, nearly lost her scholarship, and then made the biggest mistake of her life. She said yes to a date with Chris Kingsly.

Shivering, Lara brought her thoughts back to the present, wrapping her robe tighter around her. All her pain, her loss, began with Adam Govain's decision to leave her. And now he was back in her life.

TWO WEEKS LATER, ADAM took a swallow of bourbon as he paced the family room at the ranch. He still didn't know how to encourage Lara to open up to him. Surely their past relationship counted for something. Though they were young, they had truly loved each other. Leaving her had been the hardest thing he'd ever done. It had taken years to get her out of his head.

Caleb walked into the room. "What's up little brother? You look loaded for bear."

Adam stopped pacing. "Just a bit uptight, is all." He paused. "You remember Lara and I dated in high school, right?"

"Sure do."

"She wanted me to apply at University of California where her scholarship was so we could be together. I was desperate to go to Boston University so that I could work at Boston Medical Center as a medical student and do my residency there at the Trauma Center. You know how amazing that place is."

Caleb nodded. "I remember there was trouble between you two."

Adam huffed and his mouth quirked. "If you remember Lara at all, then trouble doesn't begin to describe it. She's not a person of frail emotions. She couldn't understand why I didn't love her enough to go to California. Her family needed the scholarship, whereas, she said our family would pay for me to go to the school of my choice, which was, of course, true. No matter how I explained the importance of the Boston Trauma Center experience to my dream of becoming a trauma surgeon, she still believed I could find something comparable in San Diego and that I didn't really love her. We parted with her bitterly angry with me."

Caleb squeezed his shoulder. "That must have been hard, brother. But I had no idea things were that bad between the two of you."

Adam walked over to the bar to fix Caleb a drink. "She may still be mad at me. I need to find out. What I felt for her when I was eighteen, it's like, right here." He slapped his chest.

"Well, call her."

"I don't have her number. She has mine, but I doubt she'll get in touch." Adam handed his brother his drink.

Caleb gestured with his glass. "Wait. I have it. Since we're clients, her assistant just emailed a letter to us about Lara taking over her father's practice, and it had her cell on it."

Adam grinned. "Good thinking, brother," and followed Caleb into the office.

While his brother pulled up the file on the computer, Adam created a new contact on his phone for Lara.

Caleb said, "Here it is," and stepped away.

Adam quickly typed in the number and saved the contact. "Thanks, Caleb."

Eve knocked on the open door. "Dinner's ready, you two."

Adam smiled. His brother was one lucky man. Not only was Eve a dynamic business woman with her own ranching consulting business, she was gorgeous. Her long tawny hair was perfect for her naturally tan-colored skin tone. Golden eyes gave her an exotic look and, just because she was his adored sister-in-law, he didn't dream of her sensuous mouth.

Caleb caught him watching Eve walk away and grinned. "You'll have a beautiful woman of your own someday, brother. Quit crushing on mine."

Adam laughed and followed Caleb to the dining room. Annie, their cook from childhood, was setting food on the table. She'd stayed on at the ranch house while Roy and Millie hired someone else to cook for them at the garden home they'd built not far from the main house after Caleb and Eve married. Adam came to the ranch for dinner regularly, and Annie never failed to greet him with a hug.

Caleb talked about business at dinner, and Adam asked Eve about her next training seminar. Abi laughed and played with her food from her booster seat hooked to the table top. Eve slipped spoonfuls into the little girl's mouth in between giggles and indecipherable words. Adam's parents, Roy and Millie, who came over for dinner when Adam was invited, adored Abi and talked baby talk to her like the doting grandparents they were. Normally Adam loved having dinner with Caleb and Eve, but tonight, he couldn't think of anything but getting home and contacting Lara.

As soon as politely possible, he said his goodbyes and headed to Ft. Stockton. He'd never bought a house since moving back to Texas, always thinking that at some point, he would move to a big city and work at a hospital with a Level I trauma center. So, the high-end rental he had suited his needs. The beautiful twenty-foot by forty-foot cobalt blue infinity pool edged in natural grey slate had been a definite selling point.

He enjoyed the exercise it gave him in between his busy work schedule.

Back at home, he changed into shorts and sat with a drink in the dark on the back patio, considering his options. Should he call Lara or just send a text? He wanted to talk to her. Hearing her cool, contralto voice at the reception had sent desire thrumming through him. It had always set him off. As skittish as she seemed, a text would probably be better, though. Pulling up her contact, he typed:

> *Lara, Adam here. Caleb gave me your number. I hope you don't mind. I can only imagine how hard it is to lose such a wonderful father. I'll face that myself someday, and I dread the pain of it. You've been on my mind. More accurately I should say, I can't keep my thoughts from you. Lara, I hate how things ended between us so long ago. Your parents wouldn't give me your number when I called. Now that I've found you, it's like I'm eighteen again. I want—no I need—to talk to you. Will you ... please?*

He sent it before he could change his mind. A moment later the status changed to *read*. Now that was one more thing he knew about this older Lara. She must have an iPhone too. He stared at the screen, waiting a minute, then another. Nothing happened. She wasn't answering him. His gut churned. She had to. She couldn't ignore him. Gulping the last of his bourbon, he strode into the house to make another drink.

Outside again, he paced the yard, lit only by the recessed lights of the pool. The sound of the pool's natural rock waterfall usually relaxed him, but not tonight. Bending down, he pulled a weed from the base of a large stone bird bath. The sonar sound of his text alert went off. Pulse racing, he opened the message screen. He let out a whoosh of air when Lara's name popped up.

> *Adam, I wouldn't wish the loss of a parent on anyone, yet I am coping. Thank you. I get it about being eighteen again. I feel it, too, and it makes me terribly sad. I don't want to revisit that time of my life. Please understand. Lara*

She was sad? He had to talk to her.

> *Lara, I hate it that you're unhappy. Let me see you—speak with you. Please.*

He stared at the screen as if intense scrutiny would make her reply. Minutes passed and still nothing. Returning to his seat on the patio, he laid the phone on the table and took a long swallow of his drink. Times like this were when he envied people who smoked. His nerves jittered, keeping him on a knife's edge of anticipation. What would he do if she didn't get back with him? He couldn't let her go. A high-pitched text tone came from his phone.

> *Hearing from you—seeing you—brings back my past, Adam. I put that pain behind me so long ago, and now, with you, it surrounds me again. I'm not angry. I'm not that young girl who couldn't understand your*

choice anymore. I'm happy that you've become the per-
son you wanted to be.

He turned this new information over in his mind and couldn't make sense of it. If she wasn't angry, where did her pain come from?

"I'm sorry you're hurting. I want to help. I think if you
spend some time with me, I can make things better. It
would mean so much to me, Lara.

Holding his breath, he waited for a response, but none came. He exhaled, setting his phone down. He'd pushed too hard. In silence, he finished his drink. As he stood to go inside, his text tone sounded.

Coffee? I'm in court Thursday but otherwise I'm free.

He thrust his fist in the air. Yes!

I'm off tomorrow. How about Brown's Cafe by your
dad's office? Three o'clock?

Standing in place, he waited.

See you there.

Pulse racing, he changed into swim trunks and dove into the pool, slicing through the water, covering the length in seconds. Turning, he headed back, making lap after lap, until the energy her acceptance had given him had passed.

Relaxed now, he could think. Lara had offered him a tiny opening. With it, his quest for the key to her past began.

Chapter Three

LARA ARRIVED EARLY at Brown's Wednesday afternoon, needing to find an internal calm before Adam walked in. Plagued by mistakes all day, she hoped getting this meeting under her belt would set her back on track.

When the waitress put water and a menu in front of her, Lara said, "I'm expecting a friend as well." Friend was a polite word, but was he a friend, really? Their parting years ago wasn't friendly. She took a sip of water. Maybe, after all this time, he could become a friend. It was up to her to decide if she wanted to give him that chance.

A moment later, the woman brought another water and menu.

Lara thanked her and looked out the cafe window in time to see Adam stepping out of his truck. Her heart slammed her chest wall, then picked up speed. Today he wore slacks and a dress shirt with the sleeves rolled back. How could casual be so damn sexy on a man? But that was Adam. He oozed sensual. His dark eyes, now narrowed in the sunlight, could see into her soul. No one had ever known her like Adam had. She shivered and clasped her hands in her lap, looking down. This meeting was such a bad idea.

Footsteps approached, and she looked up, her gaze snared by piercing brown eyes. "Hello, Adam."

Sitting down, he reached across the table. "You okay? Something wrong?"

"No. I'm fine." She sucked in a breath. Having him here so close—his scent, his powerful body, his voice—they were overpowering. With forced calm, she said, "Did you work today after all?"

Glancing down at his clothes, he said, "I stopped by the hospital for a few minutes before I came here. I'm the ER Department Head so when things come up, even if I'm off, sometimes I need to go in."

"Congratulations. I didn't realize that."

The waitress came by, and Adam ordered their coffee, asking Lara, "Would you like dessert?"

"Oh, no, thank you." Her body buzzed like a power line. Having him so close set off every nerve she had. Her body didn't feel friendly at all.

Adam opened his napkin, refolded it, and put it under his spoon, fidgeting.

That wasn't the Adam she remembered. He had always been so sure of himself.

"Lara, thanks for agreeing to meet with me." Pausing, he picked up his spoon, and laid it down again. "I called you. Back then. Your parents wouldn't give me your number."

She took a drink of water. "I told them not to."

"They said that." He picked up his fork and stabbed designs into his napkin. "It took me years to get over you, Lara. At least, I thought I got over you. Now that I'm with you, I don't think I ever did."

A sick feeling hit her stomach. What if she'd heard those words years ago? At the beginning? She might have made a different decision. He would have left school—

messed up his life. And for what? Their baby died.

Returning her hands to her lap, she met his gaze. "Adam, I'm sorry I was so awful to you before you went to Boston. It was incredibly selfish of me."

He reached across the table again. "No, I understood where you were coming from. But I didn't want to break up. We could have gotten together at Christmas and in the summers for a week or two. We could have worked it out."

She sighed, remembering the pain of letting him go, and shook her head. "Adam, I'm quite sure you haven't changed. You're a driven, highly-focused individual. You would have tried hard to make our relationship work, yet, maybe not the first year, but the second or third, school would have won out. Unlike you, I knew that. I couldn't bear to lose you by inches. I chose the more brutal way—all at once."

The waitress set cups in front of them and poured their coffee.

Lara added sugar and cream to hers. She concentrated on stirring so she didn't have to look at him. "So, you've become a successful surgeon, just like you planned."

Adam smiled. "Boston gave me an amazing start. During medical school, I was able to work in the Trauma Center at Boston Medical and was lucky enough to be accepted for my residency there. When I started my career, the hospital hired me. The Trauma Center is a state-of-the-art facility, and I worked with some renowned surgeons."

The joy on his face as he spoke of his early career confirmed the rightness of her decision to keep her pregnancy a secret. "What brought you back to Texas?"

He took a swallow of coffee. "Dad had a heart attack. A serious one. After that, I didn't feel right living so far from my family anymore. The hospital here had an opening, and I took it."

Her nerves had settled some. Learning about Adam and his success released the tightness in her chest. A smoky curl of sadness wound its way through her. Her life might have been so different. She sipped her coffee. "Our little St. Anne's Hospital must be quite a change after your trauma center."

Adam laughed softly. "I admit it was a shock. When I first got here, St. Anne's was only a level IV trauma center. In other words, we basically did triage and shipped our patients to a larger hospital."

Her old Adam, the whole-hog enthusiastic one, spoke now, and she swallowed a smile. "What did you do?"

He drank some more coffee, and his phone rang. Glancing at the number, he frowned and declined it. "I spent time becoming familiar with the setup, and came up with a plan. After gaining approval from the board, I enticed a friend of mine from medical school to move down here. He's an anesthesiologist and was going crazy with the pace he kept in Boston. In addition, his wife wanted him to spend more time with his family. Then I hired another ER doc—a young man just starting his career. Adding these two to our existing team gave us a much more robust response capability. Finally, I increased the education for the nursing staff and other personnel on the trauma team. We now treat most traumas on site and are ranked as a Level III Trauma Center."

"That's wonderful, Adam. The hospital is lucky you chose them." He was an amazing man, but then she'd always known that. Losing him nearly cost her her mind. She looked down at the table as her heart beat dragged. The what-could-have-beens overwhelmed her. Pushing her cup away, she said, "I need to get back to the office. I enjoyed visiting with you, Adam." Reaching into her purse, she pulled out her wallet.

His broad hand covered hers. "Lara, I've got this." He paused. "I did all the talking this afternoon. Let me take you to dinner. I want to hear about you."

A stab of dread hit her, taking her breath away. "That would take two sentences. My life is unbelievably boring."

He continued to hold her hand. "Still, say you'll come. It would mean the world to me."

God, nothing had changed. The man still drew her like iron to a magnet. She could never resist him. He'd said he felt like he was eighteen. Being with him now, she was a teenager again. She remembered her bare body laying against him. His large hands caressing her, knowing just how to awaken her passion—his gentle kisses turning into raw, hot exchanges of pure lust as they made love in the back of his truck.

But, delving into her past, their first year apart, that she wouldn't, couldn't do. "Adam, if I say yes, we don't go back to the past—to when we left for college. Okay? That time—those years—they're too painful for me. Promise?"

He went still, his eyes traveling over her face, as if looking for answers. "Agreed. For now. Are you free Saturday night?"

She nodded.

"I'll pick you up at eight."

She walked out of the cafe, mixed up, screwed up, and unable to believe she'd said yes to dinner with Adam. The man was her kryptonite. All of her woman power melted into a puddle of goo around him. Damn, she hoped he kept his promise. She desperately needed the past to be the past again.

LATER THAT EVENING, Adam pulled himself out of the pool and walked to the table for his towel. He'd expected the swim to take his whirling thoughts from Lara, but it hadn't worked. As he dried off, he picked up his phone to check for messages. *Dammit!* Demi had called again. The woman blew up his phone with texts. Today alone, he'd declined six of her calls. He dreaded the scene she would make when he told her that he wouldn't be seeing her anymore. After fixing a drink, he dialed her number and went back out to the patio.

She answered. "Adam, why didn't you pick up my calls? I tried to reach you all day."

"I couldn't have this conversation while I was at work."

"I texted you, too. Couldn't you even text?"

He blew out a breath. "Listen, Demi, we've always had a good time together. But I was honest with you. You don't want kids and I do. I like you, but I'm ready for something else now."

"What?" Breathing heavily, she said, "You can't just dump me, Adam. We've been seeing each other for months."

"Demi, look—"

"No, you look, you bastard, you can't throw me away like trash. I—"

"I don't think you're trash, Demi, I like you. I just don't want to see you anymore."

"You used me, you sorry—"

Losing all patience, he said sharply, "I used nobody. I was honest from the start, and you were perfectly happy with our arrangement. We've been fuckbuddies, at best, Demi, so don't act like it was anything more. You're a nice person, and I don't want to hurt you. Let's leave it there."

He knew she wouldn't take him turning her down well. He was angry, but a little sorry for her, too. She wore her emotions loud and proud, just like Lara used to when she was young. It was probably what had attracted him to Demi to begin with. That and her rocking hot body.

He remembered meeting Demi at a bar on an evening when he'd felt down and at loose ends. She took him home with her. That night he told her how beautiful she was, and she straight up told him she didn't want kids—that they ruined a woman's body. He said he wanted children. Pushing him down on the bed, she said, "That doesn't mean we can't have fun, honey." So, take advantage of Demi? No, he hadn't.

Swallowing his bourbon, he leaned back in the chair and consciously relaxed his muscles, glad the difficult conversation was behind him. With Demi's looks, another man would be sharing her bed in no time.

His phone screen brightened. A work email had just come through. He picked up the phone and scanned the message. It could wait until tomorrow. Tapping the phone against his chin, he considered calling Lara. It was only a little past eight. She'd be up. She still didn't seem very comfortable speaking to him, though. Sighing, he opened a text message.

Lara, I look forward to resting the first day of my time off, but this evening my thoughts are chaotic—memories of you flashing through my mind. I hold you, love you, and what I feel for you is real. It's all so strange. I'm happy, Lara, for the first time in a long time. Because you're here.

Taking a swallow of his drink, he enjoyed the warmth of it as it slid down to his belly. Sending the text relieved him somehow. She might not want to talk to him yet, but being able to express what was happening to him unwound the knot that had been in his chest for weeks. He slouched down in the chair and leaned his head on the back. He'd go out to the ranch while he was off and help Caleb. Getting on a horse always cleared Adam's head, and he liked the work.

His message tone dinged.

Adam, you were so good to me. I remember that and how much I loved you. You made my body sing. Then I remember other things, and it hurts so badly. I can't revisit that time of my life without pain. Yet, I'm happy to see you and how successful you are and the joy your career brings you. Leaving for Boston was the right choice for you.

He answered, typing swiftly:

I'm not so sure about that now. I should have searched for you. It's killing me that something so terrible happened to you that you can't bear it, even today. I should have been there for you. I should have helped you.

It took a while, but, at last, she answered.

It was my decision to face it alone.

His fingers raced across the keys.

Face what? Tell me?

Nothing. He waited as minute after minute passed. Restless, he downed the last of his bourbon. His phone sounded.

It doesn't matter now. Honestly. Good night, Adam.

He shoved himself up from the chair. *Dammit to hell!* What had happened to her? It did matter. Striding back and forth across the patio, he tried to envision what had hurt Lara in the years after their separation. She obviously did well in school. That couldn't be it. She didn't appear to have had an accident. What was it? Had she been in a bad marriage? Shit, he should have asked when he had the chance today. Instead he talked all about the great Adam Govain. He grimaced and stalked in to make himself another drink. Usually one or two drinks a night was his limit. He'd exceeded that lately. Taking a long swallow, he headed in to shower. He couldn't bear the thought that something in Lara's past still caused her such pain. At some point, he would find out and do everything in his power to take that pain away.

Chapter Four

LARA FOCUSED AGAIN on the judge. *Dammit!* This was important. Her mind couldn't wander like this. Her client needed her to give her full attention to the proceedings, and that just wasn't happening. One thing she'd always been able to take pride in was her presence in the courtroom. She awed juries and wooed judges; her clients reaped the benefits.

Lara nodded, accepting the judge's rebuke. "Yes, Your Honor." Sitting down, she glanced at her client, determined that Adam Govain would not interfere with her performance again today.

Three hours later, she left the courtroom accompanied by her client. The day had gone well for the man. He received what they asked for in the settlement. It only took two hours for the jury to decide. She'd proven beyond doubt that the other driver had clearly been at fault in the accident. Her father would have been proud that she represented his client so well.

Outside on the steps, the man shook her hand, and she strode to the parking lot for her car, relieved that she hadn't dropped the ball on the guy. She'd been damned sloppy there at the first and could not afford to let that happen again.

Adam had said what he felt for her was real. Despite her efforts to deny it, the love she'd held for him was beating at the doors of her heart. The harder she fought to keep it in the past, the more visions of him bombarded her brain. The resulting chaos had caused her foul-up in court today.

Wrenching her car door open, she slipped inside and leaned her head back. Eyes closed, she took a few moments to center herself, envisioning quiet scenes from her last fabulous vacation in Bali. She imagined tranquil beaches, the green terraced hills of a traditional village, the gentle waters of hot springs, and snorkeling in the exotic colors of the lagoon. Exploring Bali on her own had been a balm to her soul, and she'd come back to her high-stress job in San Diego completely relaxed. Maybe she could do something similar soon. Obviously, the pressure of taking over her father's business and supporting her mom was affecting her.

Arriving back at the office, her assistant, Beverly, was preparing to leave. "Lara, I put your messages on your desk, and there are a few documents for you to review and sign as well. I'll see you in the morning."

"Thank you. Good night." Normally Lara would stay and work until seven or so, but tonight she couldn't face it. Taking today's casework out of her briefcase, she loaded a couple of the files from her desk and logged off her computer. If only the Chinese place in town offered delivery. Calling in her order, she locked up and headed for her car.

By the time she got home, the first thing on her mind was a hot bath. The Chinese food she'd picked up could wait. After starting the water, she opened a bottle of wine and poured a glass. Walking to the door, she grabbed the mail she'd stepped over earlier and sorted through it. Adam's handsome face flashed before her. *Dammit!* She hadn't thought of him since her calming exercise in her car after court.

She glanced at her watch. Five forty-five. What did he do on his days off? In high school he'd always worked on the ranch. Thoughts of his lean, strong hips straddling a horse set her insides fluttering. Would she always react to the man this way? Damn, she was a train wreck when he was around. Her nerve endings turned into alien things, scooping up his essence and returning it to her a thousand-fold until she felt him in every pore of her being. While sitting across from him in the diner, his sweet, spicy scent coupled with his smooth baritone voice had overwhelmed her.

Her bath! Dumping the mail on the table and grabbing her wine, she raced to the bathroom and turned off the water. After stripping, she grabbed her phone and wine glass and slipped into the water. She liked her bath hot, and this was steaming. Her skin quickly turned pink. Sliding down until only her head and knees were above the water, she closed her eyes and breathed in the warm humid air. A memory flashed through her mind and she smiled. Without really thinking about it, she picked up her phone and texted:

> *Remember when we went skinny dipping at the pond by your house? Your parents took Dylan with them to a cattle sale, and Caleb was out with one of the herds. It was so hot that day we had to swim to the center to find cool water.*

Adam replied immediately:

> *I remember skinny dipping with you, but the water temperature isn't what sticks in my mind.*

She laughed. No, probably not. They'd made love, floating lazily in the water, sweet kisses making the day sizzle even hotter. Using a condom in the pond had been a new experience for him.

> *LOL. I hope I didn't interrupt you at something. I'm taking a very hot bath and that memory popped into my head because of the water that day.*

His answer came quickly.

> *You know I'm thinking of you in that bathtub right now.*

Damn.

> *Sorry.*

He replied.

> *Are you kidding? LOL. I've been thinking about you all day anyway.*

So, he had the same problem she did.

> *I nearly jacked up my court case today because of you. I need you out of my head!*

Her pulse sped up. Adam had taken over her brain, and she had a heart with a mind of its own. Her body reacted to him without her permission. She was out of control.

He replied:

I get it. What I feel for you—my thoughts of you—it overwhelms me sometimes. It's too new. I'm used to being alone.

What he felt for her ... what she couldn't help feeling for him. She laid her phone down and sank further down in the bath, listening to the sounds under water. For some reason this had always given her comfort. When she rose again, her heart had slowed. Slicking her hair back and then wiping her eyes, she picked up her phone again.

I've been alone a very long time, and I chose to live that way. What's happening to me now—it's rattling the doors of my safe place, and I'm not sure I can take that.

His answer flew back.

You're safe with me. I promise. Whatever it is, I'll take care of you. I'll handle it. You're not alone anymore.

She read it, and read it again as tears formed in her eyes. He would handle it? What would he think when he found out about their baby? That she didn't tell him? That she lost their little girl? He'd blame Lara as she blamed herself. She couldn't bear that.

Sinking to the bottom of the tub, she let her tears mingle with the water, wishing her guilt could so easily be washed away.

THE NEXT DAY, ADAM threw a roping saddle over the back of a tall bay gelding. He and his brother and a couple of the other cowboys were headed out to one of their herds in the part of the ranch that lay in Brewster County to rope a sick cow and her calf and bring them back to the barn.

Adam drew the cinch tight as his mind chewed over his text conversation with Lara the night before. Why did she need a safe place? And why didn't she answer back after he offered his help? Looping the cinch strap through the saddle's D ring, he secured it in a flat knot. After buckling the back cinch and the breast collar, he led the gelding outside and loaded him into the stock trailer.

Lara had been as flighty as a new-born filly since their first meeting, as if fleeing were constantly on her mind. She kept her shield up around him. He wanted to tear it down, get close to her, find out what had changed his outgoing, happy girl into this pensive, withdrawn young woman.

After Caleb loaded his mare, the other cowboys loaded their horses. The four men climbed into the ranch's double-cab truck and headed out.

Caleb drove and, once he was out on the main road, asked, "You enjoying your cowboy day, doc?"

Adam smiled. "I like keeping my hand in. I can't let you have all the fun, brother."

Caleb grinned and turned left onto the road that would take them out of Jeff Davis County and into Brewster County.

One of the cowboys had a pretty good idea where the Black Angus herd should be and, once they arrived at the right section of the pasture, it wasn't too long before they found the cattle. The sick cow the hand had spotted yesterday would be easy to pick out. She had a huge abscess on her jaw, either from a snake bite or an injury; they would find out soon enough.

After they unloaded the horses from the trailer, Adam climbed on his gelding. One of the cowboys took out a sack of feed and rattled it, before spreading piles of feed out. The cattle trotted over. Caleb, Adam and the other cowboy, now mounted, moved out, each monitoring a side of the herd in hopes of keeping them bunched. Once the ranch hand threw the feed sack in the truck and mounted his horse, Adam, who had spotted the sick cow, rode slowly into the herd, his loop thrown over his shoulder, at the ready.

As he neared the cow, she raised her head. Good girl, he thought as he swung his loop once, landing it perfectly over her head. The cow yanked backwards.

Cattle scattered, startled, and Caleb moved in. They couldn't leave the cow's calf behind. With a quick toss of his loop, he caught the calf's head and dallied his rope to the horn. The herd trotted off, the commotion too much for them.

Adam ran his horse up to the open stock trailer, pulling the cow. As his horse jumped into the trailer, he grabbed the overhead pipe and bailed off. Once the cow had been dragged inside, his gelding turned and ran back out the gate as Adam slammed it shut and removed the rope. With such a well-trained horse, a loading pen was unnecessary.

Caleb quickly loaded the cow's calf and removed Adam's rope from her head.

After pushing the cattle into the front compartment of the trailer, they loaded up the horses and headed back to the barn to wait for the vet due out that afternoon to treat the cow's abscess. After a week or two in the pen for medication, one of the hands would take her back out with the herd.

On the drive to the barn, Adam relaxed into the seat of the truck. There was something satisfying about this kind of work. It was simple. It had one outcome. No one's life depended on it. Yet, a man could go to bed at night knowing he'd done well. And the task they'd just completed had saved this cow's life. Eventually she would have become septic and died.

He compared how he felt now to how he felt after a day of work at a real trauma center, like in Boston. By the time he got home from one of his shifts, he was physically wrung out and mentally spent. And losing a patient was hard. He never got used to it and usually second-guessed himself for most of the night after a death. There was definitely something to be said for ranch life.

Once back at the barn, the cowboys handled the stock, and Caleb and Adam walked back to the house.

Abi's sitter was at the house with her while Eve presented a seminar. Caleb went to check on the little girl as Adam walked into the kitchen. "Hey, Annie. Do you have a cold glass of iced tea for a hard-working cowboy?"

She gave him a hug. "You sit yourself down at that table, and I'll bring you one. How are you, honey?"

When she handed him his tea, she took his chin in her hands and inspected him, turning his face side to side. "There's something different about you. What's going on?"

Annie had always had the sharpest eyes in Texas. She knew when he'd been up to no good and when he was hurting. He sighed. "Lara's back in town, and something's wrong with her. She won't tell me what."

Annie nodded. "And you still love her. You were always true blue. You sure this isn't about her daddy dying?"

He shook his head. "No, it's something else. From the time after we broke up. She won't talk about it."

Annie sat at the table and drummed her fingers. "I hate to see that. Lara was always such a bright, happy child. Does she still love you?"

"I don't know. I can't tell. She's all mixed up right now." Just thinking she might not hurt like hell.

Annie wiped invisible crumbs from the table with her apron. "Well, you love her. You show her that. If she's hurting, her heart may not be ready. Don't give up on her. I'll bet that sweet girl we knew is still in there."

Adam stood and gave Annie a hug. "Thank you. When I was little, if I'd lost mother, you would have been the mom I picked."

Annie smiled and shooed him out of the kitchen.

As he strode to the front door, he knew what he had to do—light a path for Lara. Help her find her way out of the safe place—the mental prison she'd created to protect herself—and into the safety of his heart.

Chapter Five

LARA LOCKED THE FRONT door, her pulse racing, like it did every time she stood near Adam.

He set his hand low on her back, escorting her to his truck.

Shivers traveled up and down her spine, his evocative scent filling her nostrils. As he assisted her into her seat, the hand he placed at her hip sent a flood of warmth to her core. Her body knew this man—his touch—and wanted more. He was bringing her back to life, and facing the consequences may be more than she could bear.

Dinner would be at the steakhouse in town, and the tight knot in her stomach didn't bode well for her chances at eating such heavy fare.

Adam glanced at her as he started the engine. "You look beautiful tonight. I've always loved you in red." White teeth flashed as he smiled the smile that had always melted her heart.

"Thank you."

He turned his attention to the road, but not before running his gaze over her again, caressing her with his eyes.

He'd always made her feel wanted and desired. She never should have dated Chris Kingsly. She should have known that there was no other man for her but Adam.

He glanced at her again. "What did you do today?"

The deep tone of his voice stroked her frazzled nerves. "I worked most of the day. Stepping into dad's practice is a little overwhelming. He had a busy case load, and I need to review each open file from the beginning to get up to speed before I can work with it."

"I'm glad we're going to dinner, then. You should relax, and put that all behind you tonight." He smiled again and she felt the warmth of it sweep through her.

She picked up her evening bag as he pulled into the restaurant parking lot. His hand sent tingles up her arm when he helped her out of the truck. As he set his fingers at her waist again, nerves fired up and down her backside. It would be so easy to lean her head into his chest—nestle into his embrace.

He opened the glass front door and a slight pressure from his hand urged her inside. After a short wait, the hostess seated them at a table with a window. Picking up the wine list, he said, "Would you like steak tonight? I was thinking of ordering a red."

She evaluated her tummy. It had settled some and she was actually hungry. "Yes, that sounds wonderful."

When the waitress returned with water glasses, he ordered a bottle of cabernet sauvignon. He smiled, his gaze sweeping over her, as if he couldn't get enough.

When their wine came, their waitress poured them each a glass and Adam raised his to her. "To tonight, and making new memories together."

Her breath hitched. Did she dare make new memories with him? Would her secret—her agonizing past—be safe? She held her glass to his. This was dangerous ground, but as she looked at the handsome, gentle man across from her, she couldn't bring herself to regret it.

While they ate, with voice lowered, Adam told her of some of the funny cases that had come through the ER. A vibrating pleasure ring stuck on a man's engorged penis. And, yes, those little blue pills can really cause a trip to the emergency room.

Trying not to laugh, she enjoyed his stories, and even more, the look of joy on his face as he spoke of his work.

He said, "Tell me about your job back in San Diego."

After a long swallow of wine, she set her knife and fork on the edge of her plate. "I was a trial attorney for criminal cases. As exciting as that was, occasionally, it made me unhappy. I was good at it, and if the prosecutor wasn't on the ball, sometimes my clients got away with murder, literally."

She took another sip of wine, knowing many people would judge her for this. "Of course, I wouldn't know if they were guilty or not when I took a case. It was only after—when I'd hired investigators and obtained all the evidence—that I would see the whole picture. Then it was pretty clear as to whether I was defending an innocent person or not. Either way, I had to defend my client to the best of my ability, with the hope that the prosecutor would do his or her job better."

Adam nodded. "That couldn't have been easy."

"No, it wasn't, but it's one of the things you need to accept if you're a defense attorney. Your client deserves the best defense in your power to give him, despite his innocence or guilt."

He smiled. "Well, I hope the pay was worth it, at least."

"It paid well. Seeing the variety of cases Dad handled and the small, in comparison, fees he charged is strange. He even did quite a bit of pro bono work, especially for young mothers.

In fact, I've gotten involved with a battered women's shelter here in town where he did a lot of his pro bono work. In San Diego, I volunteered my time at a rape crisis center and battered women's shelter, so I understand the needs of these women." Her hand tightened on the stem of her glass, swallowing hard at a terrible memory.

Chris Kingsley had been smooth—giving no hint of his cruel nature for months. After losing her daughter and suffering the crippling guilt that followed, having a man like Chris in her life seemed like a God-send. Lara had moved in with him and he made all of the decisions, handled their money, even told her how to dress. He called her every couple of hours to check on her and never left her side when he got home from work.

However, he expected her undivided attention and, over time, her grades suffered so much that her college scholarship was in jeopardy. After fixing Chris's favorite dinner one evening, she told him how she'd fallen behind in school and that she would be spending several hours each night from then on doing school work. He exploded, raping her and beating her so badly she'd lost consciousness. She found he'd gone out when she woke and she called 911.

She spent two weeks in the hospital with a broken arm and internal injuries. She'd never been able to trust enough to date a man again. Lara exhaled and pushed the memory back where it always lurked.

Unaware of her troubled thoughts, Adam continued, "Many of those battered women come through the ER. Unfortunately, they seldom press charges because of fear of the perpetrator. It's heartbreaking."

He understood. What those women faced in filing charges took incredible courage. The counseling they received at the center sometimes helped them follow through with taking legal action against their aggressor. "I just took on a big responsibility as program manager of the new clinic they're setting up at the shelter here in Ft. Stockton. As you're aware, the women often come with injuries and health problems, and their children need regular medical care as well. The clinic will also serve the low-income families in the surrounding community."

Peering over the rim of his glass, he took a swallow of wine. "So, where are you at in the planning?"

"We have the idea, and we have the space. Our grant person applied for grants last year, and we should hear back soon on those."

"So, at the beginning, really. Do you have a medical advisor yet?"

"Not per se, but we do have an RN who will work at the clinic when we open it."

He poured more wine for himself and raised the bottle. "Can I top you off?"

She held out her glass.

After pouring her wine, he said, "What if I volunteered as your medical advisor?"

She sucked in her bottom lip. That would mean working with him. Her pulse picked up. The longer she was with him, the less resistance she had to the way he affected her. But, having a medical advisor would be a fantastic benefit for the clinic. "Adam, that's a generous offer. Thank you. I'll bring it to the board and get back to you."

He shrugged. "I just want to do something to make a difference for the women I see week after week. Understanding more about the shelter and its services might help me get them out of an abusive situation. And knowing that they'll receive medical care if they do leave their relationship, will be a relief."

She leaned toward him, her lips parted. He was a man worthy of trust and always had been. It was her faith that was lacking. She had no belief in forgiveness. "You're a good man, Adam Govain."

He reached for her hand. "I'm looking forward to working with you."

The pressure of his fingers set her belly fluttering. She wanted more than this single touch. Fighting her attraction was hopeless. It wasn't just his body that made him irresistible to her. It was his beautiful soul. Sighing, she clasped his hand. "We'll make a great team."

After dinner, he drove her home and walked her to her door. As she got out her keys, he leaned his shoulder against the wall. "Invite me in, Lara."

She met his gaze. He stood there, so confident, so relaxed, so unbelievably handsome. *Oh, hell.* "Won't you come in, Adam?"

He grinned and pushed off the wall. "I'd love to."

Flipping on lights as they walked, she said, "How about wine? I have a pinot noir that would be nice tonight."

"Sure." He followed her into the kitchen and leaned against the counter, his hands in his pockets.

She glanced at him as she took glasses from the cabinet. His eyes watched her every move. Wetting her lips, she poured them each a glass. Her body revved in anticipation. But, of what? How could there be a future for them if she could never be fully honest? When she handed him the glass, his fingers grazed hers and a jolt of heat shot through her.

He smiled lazily, and she was lost.

Tingling all over, she said, "Let's go to the living room."

He followed her to the couch and sat down next to her, raising his glass, his eyes warm—his feelings for her bared. "To tonight."

Her heart slammed against her chest. What did he mean by that? Tongue stuck to the roof of her mouth, she tapped her glass to his.

He grinned and took a swallow. "Lara, I don't bite."

Letting out her breath, she sipped her wine. She was being an idiot. "I know that." With a shaky smile, she said, "I'm a little—no, a lot—out of practice at this."

He took her hand and squeezed it. "There is no *this,* there's just us. Okay?"

She nodded. "Right."

He continued to hold her hand. With only a lamp lighting the room, shadows created a warm, comfortable space around them. After another drink of wine, he let go of her hand and slid his arm around her shoulders, encouraging her to move closer to him.

Her mouth went dry. A flush of desire swept through her.

He pulled her gently into his chest and kissed the top of her head. "I've wanted to do this since I first saw you. I'll protect you, Lara." Setting his glass down, he tilted her chin so that she met his gaze. "I want to be your safe place now."

Her heart clenched with pain, sadness, but most of all regret. She blinked her eyes which threatened to overflow. He was the last person on earth who could fill that role.

"I won't pressure you." He pulled her against him again, running his fingertips slowly up and down her arm. Picking up his wine, he relaxed against the back of the couch.

The thing was, she did feel safe. At least, as long as she forgot her secret. She'd never felt more protected than when she was with Adam. She was a screwed-up mess, and had been for years. Sipping her wine, she leaned into him, her body humming in response to his caress and to what his gaze had offered her.

He finished his wine and set the glass on the table. "I'm sure you'd like to go to bed. Thanks for inviting me in." He grinned. "Not that you had much choice."

She smiled. "You're a persuasive guy."

He stood and held out a hand to help her up. "Thank you for agreeing to dinner. I know I've been persistent. But then, you know me, I go after what I want." Drawing her a step closer, he whispered, "And I want you ... no, I need you, Lara."

Standing so near, hearing those words, her resistance caved like a hollow shell. She raised her hand to his cheek, looked into his eyes and let him see her, opening the window into her pain the tiniest crack. "I've missed you, Adam."

He whisked her into his arms. "I never dreamed I'd see you again."

She slipped her arms around his neck. "I thought I'd lost you. But you're here."

He eased her back and looked into her eyes. "I'm here, baby. I'll always be here for you." Cradling her head in his hands, he lowered his lips to hers.

His gentleness aroused her more than a lust-filled kiss. He made her hunger for him—for more. She kissed him back, her tongue dancing with his.

He moaned and slid his hand to her butt, pulling her closer.

She clasped his face, tracing his lips with the tip of her tongue, then dipping inside. Teasing him, she nipped his lip and laid soft kisses along his neck, drawing him down so that she could whisper in his ear. "Thank you for dinner tonight. And, for caring for me." Her feelings too strong—too much—she placed a last kiss behind his ear, and stepped back.

He smiled, breathing quickly, no longer the in-control Adam who had strolled through her door. "I'll call you, Lara." Drawing her fingers up for a final kiss, he walked out the door.

She sighed, still standing in the spot where he'd left her. She was well and truly in it now.

Chapter Six

ADAM LEFT LARA'S HOUSE, burning with an urgent need to possess her. Leaving her after that one kiss had been nearly impossible. Only knowing that she wasn't ready for more had given him the strength to turn away. That she had returned his kiss, had let down the barrier that protected her just a little, would have to be enough, at least for now.

As he drove home, he yanked at his pants leg, giving more room at his crotch. Damn, she made him hard. That hadn't changed. Sleep tonight wouldn't come easily. He went hot at the thought of her kiss—her tongue searching his mouth. She knew what he liked. Had always known. He'd wanted to lift her into his arms and carry her to the bedroom. Make love to her until sunrise came through the window. If he gave her time—took it slow—he prayed that would happen.

Back at his house, he stripped and put on swim trunks, needing to expend the energy that burned inside him. He dove into the pool, the cold water driving thoughts of Lara from his head. Lap after lap he sliced through the water, his body an engine propelling him swiftly from one end to the other. After twenty-five laps, he stopped at the edge, gasping and free of the urge to return to Lara and coerce her into making love to him.

He climbed out and dried off. Spent, he walked in the house and made a drink. Returning to the dark patio, he slumped in a chair and let the bourbon slide down his throat, its heat dropping into his stomach, warming him, as his love for Lara warmed his heart. What a void his life had been before she returned to Ft. Stockton. She'd cracked his life wide open. Exposed it for the grey, loveless existence it was. No way could he go back to living that way. He had to break into Lara's safe place and show her that she could rely on him—love him—instead.

THE NEXT DAY, HE FREQUENTLY lost focus as he worked through his patient load. Many cases that came through the small-town ER weren't exactly emergencies but things like broken legs, which didn't tax his skills. At those times, no sooner was his task done than his mind turned to Lara—how she'd felt in his arms, the feel of her taut butt under his fingers, her soft lips on his mouth. No woman had ever affected him like this. His twelve-hour shift dragged on until he was finally able to leave at seven.

Eve had invited him for dinner at the ranch, but he'd declined, unable to face sitting still and making small talk when all he could do was think of Lara. Caleb kept him stocked with beef, so when Adam got home, he put a T-bone on the grill. Adding spices to the steak, he curled his toes, enjoying the cool slate floor of the patio. Though it was fall, the temperatures still stayed in the eighties most days. In West Texas there were really only two seasons—a little bit of winter and a whole lot of summer.

Later, after changing to his swim trunks, he flipped the meat over, more relaxed than he'd been all day. Taking his drink to the table, he flopped in the chair beside it and dialed Lara.

His heart did a flip flop when she answered. He'd yearned to hear her voice all day. If only she were with him instead of on the other end of the phone. He settled further into his chair. "How are you?"

"I'm enjoying a glass of wine with my feet kicked up on the coffee table. Now that I'm starting to get a handle on my dad's case load, I don't need to stay late at the office very often anymore."

Her contented, low-pitched voice strummed his nerves, setting them humming. Just speaking with her turned him on. "I'm glad. It can't have been easy for you." He swallowed more bourbon, easing further down in his chair.

She paused. "No, it wasn't, and seeing my mother so torn up is even harder. I'm not sure how to help her." Her voice uneven, she continued. "I see her every couple of days, and I've told her I'm here if she wants to talk. Mostly she doesn't."

God, he hated it that Lara was hurting, and he was here and she was there. "The same goes for you. I'm here if you want to talk. For anything you need."

"Thank you," she said quietly.

She seemed no closer to confiding in him. "Why don't you come for dinner tomorrow night? Wear your swim suit. I'll put something on the grill, and we'll cool off in the pool."

Again, she paused. A full twenty seconds later, she said, "What can I bring?"

He laughed, almost giddy at the thought of having her here, alone with him at his home. "Not a thing." And it was true. Lara Cole was all he needed.

"Any particular time?"

He grinned. Was now too soon? "How about seven forty-five?" Thank God she'd agreed to come. He ate quickly and changed into street clothes again, heading to the grocery store for tomorrow's dinner ingredients. Lara's slight figure told him that she usually ate light, so he returned home with items to make something he hoped would appeal to her tastes. Now he had to make it through another whole day before he could see her again.

They'd shared one kiss. He'd make sure they took another step toward intimacy before she left at the end of the night. Eventually, she would tell him what hurt her. He would break down her barrier, one brick at a time.

After putting on a pair of shorts, he mixed himself a drink and sat on the patio. Tomorrow night, he wanted more than a single kiss. Would Lara want that too? An onslaught of memories of Lara in a bikini hit him. Her ripe young body had given meaning to the word curve. The weight of her full breasts had strained the strings of the top that tied behind her neck. Did she still wear a bikini? God, he hoped so. His heart kicked up its beat as he envisioned her wearing one now. He licked his lips and took a last swallow of bourbon before heading into the kitchen to prep dinner for tomorrow.

WHEN THE DOORBELL RANG the following evening, Adam threw his tea towel on the counter and went to answer the door, eager to set eyes on Lara. He opened it to a vision from his dreams. She stood before him in cut offs and a t-shirt. Was that a bikini tied around her neck? A backpack hung from one shoulder and her long, dark curls fell down her back.

"Come in. Dinner's ready to go on the grill. I hope you're hungry." He couldn't take his eyes from her.

She smiled. "I am," and stepped inside.

He walked behind her, taken back thirteen years, as her sexy ass swayed in her denim short-shorts, her long, beautifully-shaped legs snagging his gaze. Damn, she was still hot as hell.

"Take a left up ahead," he said, "Let me get you some wine. I opened a bottle of Chardonnay in the kitchen." After pouring two glasses, he took the bag of shrimp out of the fridge and dumped the marinade in the sink. Quickly adding the ingredients to the kabob sticks, he handed Lara a glass of wine and led her to the patio.

She walked into the yard and stood on the slate walkway that edged the pool. "Adam, this place is gorgeous, and what a wonderful pool. I love the cascading waterfall. It sounds lovely."

He talked as he laid the kabobs on the fire. "I spend a lot of time out here. It's relaxing, though I feel guilty about the amount of water it takes to keep everything green. Walking on grass is such a luxury. If you remember, everything at the ranch was xeriscaped, using very little water. That's what my parents believe in."

"Do you care for all of this yourself or do you have help?"

"I have a yard man and a pool man. That way I can spend my time actually enjoying myself out here." Closing the lid on the grill, he walked out to stand beside her. "Dinner will be ready in a few minutes. The kebobs don't take long to cook." He wanted to slip his arm around her shoulders and pull her close. Even more, he wanted to nuzzle her neck and nip her behind that perfect little ear the way he knew drove her wild. He moved a little closer.

She didn't seem to mind his nearness and smiled up at him as she said, "I heard back from the board. They're thrilled with your offer to become our Medical Advisor. Thanks again for that, Adam."

He touched her arm, his fingers buzzing at the contact. "That's great. I'd love to get my hands on a set of plans for the clinic space. Can you make that happen?"

Her eyes dilated. Lips parting, she leaned toward him a fraction. "I think so. I'll see what I can do."

He wasn't misreading. She wanted him, too. Taking her hand, he pulled her to him. Wrapping his arms around her, he hugged her gently, kissing the top of her head. "I'm glad you came tonight, Lara. Having you here with me is incredible." Her body was warm and soft, and he wanted more than just this, but knew he needed to go slow. Sighing, he released her. One brick at a time.

She stepped back, biting her lip. "I'm happy to be here." Her gaze, less guarded than before, said she was.

He smiled. "Come sit with me. I need to baste dinner or they won't taste right." He'd made a garlic oriental marinade spiked with fresh squeezed orange juice to brush the kabobs with.

As he tended to their meal, she asked, "How are your mom and dad?"

"I don't know. I skipped dinner at the ranch this week. I couldn't get you off my mind."

A pink flush rose up her neck, and she looked at her wine glass, twirling the stem. "I confess, I've had the same problem."

His pulse beat faster at her admission, and he kept up a light conversation as he basted the skewers. Taking the kabobs off the grill a few minutes later, he placed them on a platter and set them on the center of the table. After bringing the salad and bottle of wine out, he sat down beside her. Raising his glass, he said, "To us."

Her eyes widened, but she tapped his glass. "To us."

Her words, spoken quietly but with surety, gave him confidence that she had relaxed—opened herself more. His chest hardened as he thought of kissing her again. Tonight, he hoped she lowered her guard. That she trusted him enough to let him in. He handed her the plate of kabobs. "Help yourself. I've cooked these before, and they're simple, but delicious. It's only shrimp, pineapple and green pepper but the sauce infuses it with a tangy garlicy flavor."

She took one then added some salad to her plate. "So, do you eat out a lot or cook like this for yourself?" Her gaze, warm and interested, made him want to lean in and kiss her full lips. He needed her near him. Why hadn't he put the place settings side by side?

He took two kabobs and some salad and then topped off their wine. "It depends. When I'm working, I usually stop and pick dinner up, or microwave something. When I'm off, many times I'll cook." He smiled, putting all his powers of persuasion in his eyes. "You need to come over more often. I hate cooking for one."

She smiled, holding his gaze an extra beat. "I have the same problem. Cooking for just one person, it's like, why bother? Although, eating out can really add on the calories."

"*Pft*. Like you have to worry." His eyes let her know he liked what he saw.

Her tongue flitted across her lip as she looked down.

Damn, he wanted to pull her on his lap and kiss that gorgeous mouth. His hand tightened on his glass as he took a swallow of wine. He scraped the food off his skewer and picked up a shrimp, chomping it in half to distract himself.

His phone rang. *Dammit!* Demi had been relentless today, after leaving him alone for days. He declined the call, then pulled up her contact and blocked her number, which he should have done sooner, but he'd been too busy to take the time.

Lara asked, "Problem?"

He frowned. "Not anymore."

Thankfully, she talked about work and asked him about the ER, and soon they'd finished dinner.

As he stood to clear the table, she said, "Let me help."

At the sink, when her arm brushed his, tingles raced across his chest. He took her shoulders, turning her to him, looking into her eyes. Lowering his mouth to hers, he placed a tender kiss on her lips, slid down to her slender throat and kissed her in the hollow there. He didn't want to stop, he itched to remove her clothes, take her in his arms and carry her to his bed.

She clasped his face then kissed him gently. "I'm ready for that swim."

Heart racing, it was all he could do to let her go. He took her hand, "Come on then. I'll finish these later."

On the patio, he stripped off his t-shirt and couldn't help himself. His gaze locked on Lara as she pulled her shirt over her head and stepped out of her shorts, exposing a bright turquoise bikini which set off her tanned skin and dark hair beautifully. She must have gotten lots of sun in California. "You're beautiful."

She smiled. "Thanks. How deep is the pool?"

Unable to take his eyes off her, he said, "Three feet on this side, ten feet on the deep end." Dammit, he was getting hard and he couldn't hide it in a swimsuit. "Race you." He ran to the far side and dove in, Lara right behind him.

As he popped up to the surface, her head appeared a few feet away. He laughed, "Still can't turn down a challenge, huh?"

She grinned, "No way, buster." Slicking her hair back, treading water, she looked at him.

He swam to her, gazing into her eyes. "How do you like my pool?"

She moved her hands to his shoulders, "Very nice."

Slipping his hands around her waist, he pulled her to him. "I love it."

Her lips parted and she blinked slowly, staring up at him.

He brushed his lips to hers. Her mouth opened to his kiss, warm and welcoming. He explored her, tasted her, until she took control, teasing his lips with soft flicks of her tongue as he kept them afloat. Goosebumps blew up all over him. He drew her thighs around his waist, hard now and wanting her body pressing against him. She locked her legs, squeezing him and he thrust his pelvis forward without thinking.

She gasped.

He took her face in his hands, his kiss coaxing, confident as he poured everything he had into it. *Let me in. You're safe with me.*

She kissed him back, slipping her arms around his neck, her lips hungry, demanding.

Yes. Yes, Lara. He desperately wanted to make love to her, but even more than that, he needed her to know he loved her.

He pulled back. Her lips were lush and red from kissing him. "I love you. I never stopped loving you. You can trust me." He cupped her face in his hand. "I'll take care of you."

She looked into his eyes, and with the smallest of smiles, she nodded and drew him in for a gentle kiss.

He said, "Come on," and swam for the shallow end. The splash of her strokes followed him. When he got to the towels, he smiled and tossed her one. "Hurry."

She raised her brows, but complied, first wringing her hair dry in the towel, then drying her body off.

He stopped her. "We'll just get wet again."

She grinned. "What?"

He jogged to his bathroom, Lara in tow. Shutting the door, he went into the huge tile shower and turned on the big square shower head full blast, setting the temperature to warm. He'd be heating up Lara plenty. Grinning at her, he tugged down his swim trunks. "Last one in's a rotten egg."

Laughing, she ripped the bow from her top and unhooked the back, slinging it off. Down came the tiny bottoms and she stepped into the shower beside him. Bumping him with her hip, she said, "Scoot over. I'm cold."

He cracked up. "I'll heat the water more, but I warn you, you'll be asking me to turn it down, girl."

She laughed. "Really?"

"For sure."

"You never lacked for confidence, Govain."

He grinned and pulled her to him, the water plastering their hair back, his cock hard. "Don't break my heart, babe. Kiss me." He rubbed his length against her and she leaned into him. He could smell her perfume in the shower's steam. Lifting her so that she was eye to eye to him, he kissed her deeply as she wrapped her legs around his waist. God, he wanted her. He reached for the condom in the soap dish and handed it to her. "Safety first."

She smiled. "Thanks for remembering." Tearing open the package, she worked it on him, her hands shaking.

Raising her higher, he slipped his tip to her opening. It was slick—ready for him. He looked into her eyes and kissed her softly. "I love you, Lara." Lowering her slowly, he filled her completely. Damn, she was tight.

She leaned her head back and closed her eyes. He thrust his hips forward and she moaned. Grasping his face, she kissed him eagerly, nipping and sucking and dipping inside him.

The sharp need of her kiss aroused him even more. He pushed her back against the wall and thrust into her. God, she was everything he'd dreamed she would be. Pulling out, he shoved into her again.

Clasping his neck, she said, "I want you."

His heart leapt. Fire shot through his limbs. He kissed her hard, thrusting his tongue deep as he pounded her with his hips, the water splashing chaotically off his back.

"Adam," Lara's moan vibrated straight to his cock and she clutched him tight with her legs.

He drove into her, his joy, his excitement growing. His muscles knotted, pressure building, the agony of pleasure almost more than he could stand.

Lara suddenly lifted her head, sucking in a breath and calling his name. She contracted around him, spasming, and sending him over the edge.

He burst in a bone-deep growl of pleasure, thrusting one, two more times, unleashing his love into her. Head thrown back, he held still, wanting the moment to last. Myriad feelings overwhelmed him. Intense love for the beautiful woman in his arms, an overpowering sense of loss because of the years that they'd been apart, and hope that Lara loved him now, as he loved her.

A moment later, she slid her feet to the floor and grinned at him. "You've still got it, Govain." She took a wobbly step.

He reached for her elbow. "Take it easy there, cowgirl."

"Cowgirl?"

"Yeah, you just rode your big stud."

She laughed. "You'll never change."

He handed her the shampoo while he grabbed the soap. "Nope."

"I hope you have conditioner."

"The shampoo is a conditioner. Does that count?"

She sighed. "Oh, I'm in trouble. Without conditioner, combing this hair is impossible."

He leaned in and kissed her, water splashing them both in the face. "I'll help. I used to be pretty good at that, if you'll remember." He'd loved brushing her hair and running the long strands through his fingers.

Her smile gentle, she said, "I do remember that. Thanks."

Later, as she dried her hair with a towel, he said, "Can you stay tonight?"

Her eyes widened and a wariness came to her expression. "I shouldn't."

When she didn't offer an explanation, he said, "I'll go get your bag." Despite the fact that she couldn't stay, his heart was so full, so happy, he stopped a moment in the living room, letting the feeling wash over him. He hadn't felt like this since he'd last made love to Lara. His life had come full circle. Grabbing her bag, he headed back to the woman he loved.

She eyed his naked body as he walked up to her. "You're still the same—don't care if you have clothes on or not."

He grinned. "Nope."

She shook her head and smiled, opening her bag and taking out clean clothes.

He threw on some shorts and a t-shirt and climbed up on the bed, scooting until his back was against the head board. "Come up here when you're done, and I'll comb your hair."

A couple of minutes later, she settled between his spread legs.

He kissed the top of her head and took her brush from her. "Just relax, babe. I've got this."

She sighed. "I love it when you do my hair. You're so gentle. Combing out this mess is a pain in the butt, and I dread it. Thank you, Adam."

He began at the back, taking a long lock in his hand. Starting at the bottom, he brushed the tangles out, slowly working his way to the scalp. The scent of her perfume filled his nostrils, turning him on as it always had. Lara didn't have a signature perfume, but had a way of choosing those that complimented her chemistry in a striking way. Strand after thick strand, he brushed his way through her hair. Winding the silky locks through his fingers brought back lazy, loving memories of lost summer days.

Her neck and shoulders relaxed, and if she were a cat, she would have purred.

He combed through her hair one last time and kissed her cheek. "All done, my love."

She sat up straight. "You almost put me to sleep." She turned toward him and rose to her knees. Looking into his eyes, she pressed her lips to his, the kiss long and leisurely.

Desire burned through his nerves again. He wrapped his arms around her and pulled her close, returning her kiss, teasing her lips, wanting her to remember when she was gone how much she wanted him.

She drew back and cupped his face in her hands, her eyes shuttered. "Thank you for tonight, Adam. It was a magical evening." She slid off the bed and grabbed her bag.

Reaching for her hand he said, "I've got you now, Lara. I want to help. I don't want you in pain. We have to talk, sweetheart."

She lowered her eyes and drew her hand away.

He walked her to the door, his heart already missing her.

She opened it, then turned to him.

Dammit. That wariness was back in her eyes. He raised his hand in a wave. The door shut behind her, and she may as well have entered a jail cell. She was still in her safe place. Two steps forward, one step back.

Chapter Seven

LARA STRODE TO HER car, doubt whipping her like the Texas wind. For a while tonight, it had seemed like old times. Adam wasn't just her lover—he was her best friend. How easily she'd fallen back into that time and place. All the love she felt for him had filled her heart and the ecstasy of his lovemaking still rocked her.

When Adam, always the honest one, had professed his love, an unwanted crack had appeared in her protection. She ignored it, wanting him too much. When he asked her to sleep over, her world split wide open. She couldn't pretend anymore. Loving him, taking his honesty while keeping a desperate secret of her own, wasn't right. Of course, she couldn't stay. She would treat tonight as a beautiful dream. Nothing more.

Back at home, she slipped into a night gown and poured a glass of wine in the kitchen before returning to her bed. Leaning against the headboard in a room lit only by moonlight, she sipped, unable to forget the touch of Adam's hands on her body, the sensation of him inside her. He was the only man who had ever brushed her hair. The sensuous feeling of his fingers sifting through the strands had left her limp with pleasure.

Her text tone sounded, and she picked up her phone. Adam.

Lara, I can't stand this empty bed. I need you here beside me. I want you cuddled in my arms, your head on my chest, your sweet mouth near so I can kiss you goodnight. You're what's been missing from my life. I was half a man, and now I'm whole again. I sense your worry, and I'm not sure why, but I won't hurt you. I would never do that. Trust me. Trust yourself to love me as I love you. Adam

She read it again. His honesty was a knife to her chest. She couldn't match it. She would have given their baby away. Then she lost her. If Lara had been a better mother, maybe her baby girl would be alive. The years since had done nothing to ease her shame. How could she tell Adam of her betrayal—that she kept the knowledge of his daughter from him? Knowing him now, that truth would destroy him. She couldn't do it.

Adam, I don't know what I was thinking tonight. I let myself dream. I shouldn't have. You're such a wonderful man. Thank you for loving me still. But I can't go there. It's not right, and I won't do it. Lara

He responded immediately.

Why, Lara? Why isn't it right? I'll understand, whatever it is. Just tell me what's hurting you. Is it not right because you're somehow married? Help me understand. Let me be here for you, Lara. You're not alone now. You have me. I'm not going anywhere.

Married? Is that what he thought?

I'm not married. Never have been. I can't say anymore. Not to you. Not ever. Good night, Adam.

A minute later, he finally replied.

I'm glad you're not married. Good night.

She laid the phone against her chest, needing the contact with him, if only with his words. He would have wanted their daughter, but having her would have destroyed his life. Adam wouldn't be the man she knew now. She wouldn't be who she was either. But, really, was that such a loss? For years she'd thought she had it together. That her past was behind her. It only took seeing Adam Govain again to show her how wrong she was.

She emptied her glass and set it on the nightstand, the wine in her belly no comfort at all. When she'd returned to Ft. Stockton, Adam was the last person she expected to find. In her thoughts, he was always a successful doctor back East somewhere, not living here in Texas. If she had come home more frequently, her parents might have mentioned him in passing. Though she had a very busy career, that hadn't been the real reason she visited so seldom. Her memories kept her away, and she wasn't proud of the fact, especially now that her father was gone, and she'd never spend time with him again. She could add being a bad daughter alongside being a bad mother in her list of faults.

Turning over, she closed her eyes, the old hopeless feeling swallowing her. It was too bad her mother couldn't have borne more children. Here she was stuck with a useless daughter in her time of grief. As Lara had thousands of times before, she prayed, asking God for his forgiveness. If she had only wanted her baby more, or done something different, her baby girl might be alive today ....

ADAM MADE IT THROUGH his twelve-hour shift the next day like a sleep walker. Thank goodness no real traumas came through the doors. His head wasn't in the game. Lara's words reverberated through his brain. What was not right? Why couldn't she talk to him? She made it seem like it was him specifically she couldn't talk to. What the hell did that mean? And it had sounded like she was saying goodbye. He couldn't lose her now. Not when he'd found her again. He left the hospital, and though he hadn't eaten lunch, he didn't stop for dinner. His stomach was a burning bag of acid.

When he got home, he changed clothes and ate a piece of bread along with a glass of milk, coating his belly with food before fixing a drink. Clouds covered the sun and wind blew the branches of the tree in the yard. He sat on the edge of the pool and dangled his legs in the water. Taking a swallow of bourbon, he considered what to do about Lara. She was shutting him out, and he couldn't let that happen.

He picked up his phone. Eight o'clock. Dammit, he had to talk to her. He texted:

You home?

A few seconds later:

Yes.

He typed fast:

Need to see you. I went nuts all day, thinking about us and worrying about what's wrong.

He waited, but she didn't answer. Still, he stayed his fingers, giving her time. At last, she sent:

You're always so honest, Adam. Today was hard for me, too. Yet, I'm not sure seeing each other is a good idea.

He wrote right back:

Of course, it is. We belong together. Didn't you feel it last night? I did. I'm not giving up, Lara. Despite whatever problem you're facing, I'm here for the long haul.

She didn't text. He waited longer, but still nothing. Had she put the phone down? His heart lurched. A weight settled on him. What was so bad that Lara couldn't tell him? They'd always been able to talk about their troubles. They'd shared everything.

Then she texted:

This is so hard, Adam. You're a wonderful man. I don't deserve your love.

He sent:

Don't move. I'm coming over.

He threw some clothes and toiletries in a pack and slung it over his shoulder, heading out the door in less than five minutes.

LARA PACED THE LIVING room, gulping her whiskey. She feared Adam's arrival for what she knew he would ask of her, yet she welcomed it too. Her pain screamed for release. It had been too long inside her, and Adam was the one person on earth who could seize that agony and drive it from her heart. Taking her last swallow, she refilled her glass, needing every ounce of courage the liquor would give her.

The sound of Adam's truck came from her driveway. Pulse racing, she strode to the door and opened it.

Dusk had deepened the shadows and she peered through the dim light as Adam headed toward her with a quick, purposeful stride. As he got to the door, he said, "Lara," and kissed her cheek.

She stepped back, allowing him to precede her inside, her pulse beating so fast she could feel it in her neck. What would he do?

Walking to the couch, he turned to her, beckoning with his hand. "Come here, Lara."

With no thought of disobeying his command, she moved to face him and looked into his steady, demanding gaze.

Grasping her shoulders, he leaned down and captured her lips in a fervent, insistent kiss, one she responded to with an eager burning intensity. His need, his authority, overpowered her reluctance.

Her qualms about telling him the truth began to fade as he kissed her again with fiery, hot-blooded passion. She said, "Adam, I'm so sorry."

He drew her into his arms and leaned his cheek against her. "Tell me now. Tell me everything. Don't stop talking until I know it all."

He'd done it—made her ready to crack open her soul.

He pulled her down on the couch with him, wrapping his arm around her shoulders and snuggling her close. Cradling her face in his palm, pressing her into his breast, he said, "Start from the beginning, honey."

Thank God he didn't expect her to meet his gaze. Instead, she stared at her hand caressing his broad chest. "I was heart-broken when you left for Boston."

"I remember. It nearly killed me."

"When I started school, I missed two periods in a row and found out I was pregnant."

His arms clutched her tighter, and he sucked in a breath. "You didn't tell me."

She closed her eyes, her heart a heavy stone in her chest. "You had already made your decision to go to Boston—to leave me. I didn't think dragging you back with an unexpected pregnancy would be right. I didn't feel like you wanted me, or my baby, more than you wanted your Boston Trauma Center."

He raised her face to him, insisting that she look at him. "I never wanted to lose you. I loved you. I just wouldn't have been able to see you very often."

She pulled her face away. "Come on, Adam. We both know how you were. Probably still are. Driven, totally focused. Within a few years you would have let me go in favor of excelling at university. I couldn't bear the thought of losing you that way. And what about caring for the baby? Should I have given up school? Which of us would have worked to support us?"

He clenched his jaw. "I should have had the chance to choose."

Nodding, she said, "I know that now. Then, I thought it was all on me. I did what I thought best."

He exhaled loudly. "What happened to our baby, Lara?" His voice strained with the effort to say those words.

Did he hate her yet? If not, he soon would. She tucked her chin into her chest, her voice low as she said, "The campus clinic prepared me for all eventualities. I had resources for termination provided as well as information for free or sliding scale maternity care if I chose to keep the baby. I was also given brochures for several agencies if I decided to give my baby up for adoption." She sighed, her stomach a ball of lead in her belly. "I chose the last option. The agency I signed up for paid for my maternity care and expenses." How would he look at her now that he knew she hadn't wanted his baby?

She swallowed hard and tried to pull away.

Holding her firmly, he kissed the top of her head. "Go on. I'm listening," he said in a tight but gentle voice.

She couldn't bear what happened next. If only she could bypass it, she could get through the telling. She pulled back. "Adam, I ..."

He cradled her head against him. "Tell it. I won't judge you. I won't let you stop now, either."

Oh, God. How could she tell him that she should have been a better mother? That she should have tried harder, wanted her baby more—something—and maybe their baby girl would still be alive?

"I ... I loved my baby," she stammered. "Even though I signed the papers to give her away—"

He interrupted her. "Our baby is a girl?"

She bit her lip, nodding, tears beginning to form in her eyes. "I felt her first fluttering movements with such incredible joy."

His hands clenched her. His eyes drilled into her. "Where is my daughter, Lara?"

Her hand flew to her face. A sob wrenched from her throat as she whispered, "I lost her. I'm sorry, Adam."

He forced her face to him. "What do you mean? How did you lose her?"

She couldn't look at him, couldn't see the anger and revulsion that would surely be in his eyes. Eyes closed, she said, "Spontaneous abortion at four and a half months. If only I'd loved her more. If I'd wanted to keep my baby girl, it wouldn't have happened. I know that. A good mother would have taken better care of her baby. I didn't read any baby books. I didn't study how to be a good mom. I took my little girl for granted." Wrenching herself from his grasp, she wiped her tears away. "It's my fault our baby is dead."

Adam sat in stunned silence beside her.

She got up and paced the room. Her pain of a moment before was turning to a numbing hollow ache. Adam could never love her now. Never look at her the same.

He took a large swallow of his drink and met her gaze, his eyes pained, but also forgiving. She hadn't expected that at all. Rising, he intercepted her pacing and brought her back to the couch. "Lara, thank you for telling me. I was a selfish fool. You should never have had to face your pregnancy alone. My choice to go to school in Boston when I could have made school with you in California happen, took away your trust in me." He scrubbed his hand over his face. "I can see why you didn't think I'd come back." Clasping her hand, he said, "I would have. I would have wanted our baby."

She pulled her hand away. "Yes, but would you have blamed me? Blamed our little girl? I couldn't bear the thought of that. You made it clear you wanted your career as a trauma surgeon above everything. How long would it have been before you started resenting losing your dream? Which one of us would have quit school? Me or you? Someone needed to support us. Do you see what I faced? I could kill your dream or kill mine. I could have you blame me or I could blame myself for giving my baby away." Her chest clenched, and she bit back a sob. She would never get over the pain of that horrible, fateful choice.

"Come here," Adam said as he drew her into his arms again. Holding her tight, cupping her head to his chest, he said, "I'm so sorry, Lara. I can't imagine your pain. It was a terrible choice to face. I know you. You took care of yourself during your pregnancy. Do you realize that up to twenty percent of pregnancies end in miscarriage? It's most often because there's something wrong with the fetus. Honey, losing our baby wasn't your fault. You couldn't have prevented it. I'm so sorry it happened, and I know you were in agony. I don't blame you, and you shouldn't blame yourself." He brought her hand to his lips, looking into her eyes and letting his love shine a light into her devastated soul.

His steady, healing gaze poured into her heart, stealing through her cold arms and hands, relaxing her tense muscles. He didn't hate her? Didn't blame her? She closed her eyes, let herself float in the warm cocoon of acceptance his words had given her. She hadn't known so many pregnancies ended as hers did. Did those other women blame themselves too? Adam had said something else. Her baby—something may have been wrong. Lara thought of the mass she'd seen and accepted that it might be true.

Exhausted, she said, "Thank you, Adam, for understanding. I'm so sorry I didn't tell you so you could have had a choice. It was your right."

He kissed the top of her head. "Hush. You did the best you could. I share the blame for that decision. I want you to let the pain go, now. I'll help you. You don't have to face it alone anymore."

He held her for long, silent moments. Then, squeezing her shoulder, he said, "I didn't eat before I came. Have you had dinner yet?"

She nodded. "I had a salad when I got home. Would you like me to make you something?"

He smiled. "That would be great. I brought a bag. I'd like to stay and hold you tonight." His gaze locked with hers and the love, the vulnerability in his eyes sent ripples of joy through her.

"I'd love that, Adam." She kissed him, caressing his cheek, and stood. "I'll make you something. Be right back."

In the kitchen she took out ingredients for a turkey and ham sandwich, feeling light, free, like she could soar to the moon. With Adam's forgiveness, maybe she could begin to forgive herself. She wasn't a fool—it would take time—but the possibility was amazing. Finishing his sandwich, she set it in the dining room and went to get him. "While you eat, I'll shower. Come on."

As she washed her hair a few minutes later, she let her mind wander to the night to come, falling asleep wrapped in Adam's arms, feeling his hard body pressed against hers. He was so tall, she always felt tiny in comparison. Healing would be slow, but with Adam it could happen.

After her shower, she walked into the living room in her gown and robe, towel drying her long hair.

Adam had finished eating and sat drinking another whiskey. He smiled, his eyes lighting with desire. "I see I have some hair to comb out."

She grinned. "I'll take that offer. Shower's all yours. Let me show you the bathroom."

He'd brought his bag in from the truck while she showered and followed her. When she stepped aside so he could enter the room, he dropped his bag and took her into his arms. "Too bad you've already had your shower."

She laughed. "Hurry up, cowboy. I'll be waiting right here."

He smacked her butt and headed inside.

While Adam showered, she locked the doors and turned out lights. Back in the bedroom, she lit two scented candles and took off her robe before sliding into bed; the lamp on the nightstand set on low.

As he walked out of the bathroom, Adam's clean spicy scent spread through the room. His chest was bare and he wore a pair of athletic shorts.

She inhaled, and goosebumps raced up her arms. Her breasts felt swollen and her nipples pressed against the fabric of her gown. The sight of him had set her pulse racing.

He grinned and laid a condom on the table before slipping under the covers. Reaching for her, he said, "Scoot over here, darling. I need a kiss before I comb that beautiful hair."

Moving against him, she lifted her face, opening her lips.

He kissed her gently, almost reverently, running his hand up her side and cupping the back of her head, whispering, "You make me happy, Lara."

She swept his lips with a kiss. "I'm glad you stayed."

Patting her butt, he sat up. "Brush, please?"

Handing it to him, she scooted between his legs, soon losing herself to the intense pleasure his gentle hands gave her as he coaxed her tangled strands into smooth, silken curls.

Adam pulled her hair to the side, nuzzling her neck until it tickled. "All finished, love."

She turned her face for a kiss. "Thank you. That was amazing." Scooting to her side of the bed, she switched off the lamp. Her eyes adjusted to the darkness, only the two candles throwing light into the shadows of the room.

A swish of fabric sounded and she knew it for Adam taking off his shorts. She grinned. That man loved to be naked. A lusty feeling of warmth stole over her. He reached across her and a condom package tore open. He would take care of her.

He pulled her to him in the candlelight, his smile promising tenderness.

An old familiar shiver coursed through her. He was her Adam, come back to her. She slid into his arms, welcoming his touch. Heat unfurled in her belly. She needed absolution on tonight of all nights.

He drew her up, face to face and looked into her eyes, his love flowing into her in rivers of emotion. It filled her, helping to wash away the guilt and the pain. With a gentle smile, he lay her on her back. His palm held her face as his thumb caressed her lip before he brushed her lips with tender kisses. He gently removed her gown, then lay her back down again.

She was adored, cherished. His lips found her hollows, her special, sensitive places, as he brought her alive with his mouth and his touch.

As she worshiped his body, her kisses and nimble hands made him pant with desire.

She spread her thighs and he covered her, holding his weight with his arms. Guiding him in, she groaned with pleasure as he made her full and tight.

He withdrew and slowly filled her again.

She arched into him, wanting him deeper inside her.

He looked into her eyes as he entered her with slow gentle strokes, caressing her with his love.

Clasping his butt, she felt his muscles contract with each move and the evidence of his power heightened her desire.

He bent and kissed her so softly her lips tingled at the touch. A smile lit his face with a glow only true love could give.

Her heart swept open and she clasped him, bringing him to her and kissing him deeply. She looked into his soft brown eyes and said, "I love you, Adam, and I always have."

His eyes widened. He claimed her lips with abandon, sweeping her mouth with his tongue, branding her with his hot kisses. His strokes increased, swiftly pummeling her, his hips slapping against her in a staccato rhythm.

She curled her legs around his hips as he pounded her pleasure spot. Tension built inside her. She clutched him, muscles tight, sweet bliss coming to her wave after wave in time with his strokes. Moving under him, she moaned with each thrust. Teetering on the edge, she gritted her teeth. He thrust again and her orgasm crested like an ocean wave, ripples of ecstasy spreading through her. She cried out, "Adam," and spasmed around him, holding him with all her strength.

He thrust once, twice more and came with a shuddering cry.

She tossed her head, her pulse thundering in her veins. Adam lowered himself on her and kissed her lightly on the lips. Neither one of them said anything.

Soon, he pulled her into his arms to spoon against his chest and nibble at her ear. She giggled as he whispered, "Did you mean what you said?"

Knowing what he meant, she reached up to clasp his face. "Yes."

He squeezed her tighter and sighed. "Thank God. I was getting pretty desperate."

She turned to face him. "Adam Govain, I love you. Believe it."

He grinned and kissed her forehead, then cuddled her to his chest.

She lay still, filled with a peace that had been absent from her life for more than thirteen years. It felt fragile, like maybe she didn't deserve it. Like it could break any minute. Closing her eyes, she prayed that it didn't.

Chapter Eight

AS LARA PREPARED BREAKFAST, Adam enjoyed her sweet ass and sexy little feet moving briskly about the kitchen. A contentment like he'd never known eased his tense muscles and he lived this moment fully present, imprinting it on his mind as a favorite memory. He looked forward to spending lots of time with her this weekend.

She set an omelet in front of him, along with a glass of orange juice, then brought hers from the counter and sat across from him at the dining room table. "Eat up, cowboy, you've got a lot of calories to replace."

"What? I could make love to you all night with one arm behind my back."

She laughed and shook her head, taking a big bite of egg. With a full mouth, she said, "Right. My he-man."

They were back in old habits—her teasing him while he acted like a stud. She never let him get one up on her. Damn, he'd missed it, missed her, so much. He finished chewing. "Eve invited me for dinner at the ranch this evening. Come with me, Lara."

Her eyes darkened and she concentrated on her plate. "Wow. The ranch. That would be a blast from the past."

He urged, "You'll love Eve. I'm not sure if you remember her from the funeral. I couldn't ask for a better sister-in-law. And Abi, their baby girl, is the sweetest thing ever."

Lara looked up, her mouth tight. "I saw you holding her that day. I wondered at the time if she were yours."

He raised his brows. "Really?"

Nodding, her hand shook as she cut another bite of egg.

"Lara, I'm glad I never married. I'm happy I don't have children. You're the only one I want a baby with," he said firmly.

Her hand stilled, her fork half-way to her mouth. Eyes downcast, she nodded again.

He reached across the dining room table, needing to be closer to her for his question. "Lara, why didn't you marry—have children of your own?"

She put her fork down, her hands diving to her lap. Without looking at him, she said, "I made a terrible mistake."

As the story of her relationship with Chris Kingsley unfolded word by hateful word, anger roiled in his chest. When she told him about the rape, he stood so fast that his chair fell backwards, his hands balled into fists. Rushing to her side, he crouched down and pulled her into his arms. "Oh, babe, no, no." Through clenched teeth, he said, "I'll kill him. I'll find him and kill him."

She shook her head. "No, he went to jail, and I want nothing to do with him. Let it be." Pulling back, she took her napkin and blew her nose. "That's why I volunteer at the rape crisis center. I've come through it, and I want to help other women survive." Meeting his gaze, she continued. "What I didn't do, was learn to trust my intuition about men again after what Kingsley did to me. I never had the courage to trust a man, much less date. My career became my life until I moved back here."

He tucked a lock of hair behind her ear, and clasped her arm. "You won't need to worry about that anymore. You can trust me." He stared into her eyes, willing her to believe him. She nodded, and he let her go, returning to his chair. Stabbing his omelet with his fork he said, "I was a selfish fucking bastard, and I only hope, Lara, that someday you'll find a way to forgive me."

Sighing, she said. "I forgave you when I saw you again and realized what a wonderful person you've become, and what an amazing doctor you are. I knew then that my decision allowed you to grow into the best man you could possibly be. How could I regret that?"

He clenched his fork. "If I could go back, I would do everything differently. I never would have gone to Boston. I'd have gone with you to California and stayed by your side for everything that happened. We'd have found a way to make things work, and we'd have been together these past thirteen years."

She picked up her plate with her nearly untouched omelet and headed to the kitchen. "We have now, Adam. We'll make it enough."

When she walked back in, she took his face in her hands and kissed him softly. "Thank you for loving me and for saying you would have come back. I love you so, so much, Adam Govain." She kissed him again, and the trust in her eyes was a precious gift, one he didn't deserve, but one he would strive every day for the rest of his life to earn.

LARA WAITED OUTSIDE the Govain ranch front door, her pulse racing. Even Adam's arm around her shoulders didn't ease her nervousness. The last time she'd been inside this house, she was an innocent young girl with her whole life ahead of her. She'd had no idea of the heartbreak that would soon rain down on her head.

Caleb answered the door, a wide grin on his face. "Hey, you two, come on in." He reached for Lara's hand as he stepped back to allow them to enter the house. "It's wonderful to see you again. How are you all holding up?"

Feeling more comfortable after Caleb's warm welcome, she said, "I'm okay. Mom's still struggling, of course, but she's doing a little better."

"I'm glad." He squeezed her hand then turned his attention to his brother, slapping him on the back. "About time you brought a woman around. I was beginning to wonder if you'd turned into a monk."

Adam laughed. "Not a chance."

Caleb said, "Lara, Mom and Dad aren't here tonight. They're in Las Vegas. They'll be sorry they missed you."

She smiled. "I was looking forward to seeing them, too. Please tell them I said hi."

"Okay, but you need to come out again soon and tell them yourself."

As they entered the family room, Eve came toward them. "Welcome, it's so nice to see you. I want to say again how sorry I am about your dad." After giving Lara a hug, she turned to Adam. "Glad you could come. We missed you at dinner last week."

Lara didn't remember Eve from the funeral, though how she'd forgotten such a stunningly beautiful woman was hard to imagine. And Caleb—he'd grown into a tall, perfectly-honed example of a handsome cowboy. They made a striking couple.

Eve picked up the baby from the blanket on the floor where she played. "This is our daughter, Abi."

Lara smiled and reached for the baby's hand, bending to catch her gaze. "I remember this precious girl."

Abi clutched Lara's fingers and gazed into her eyes, making little sounds with her tiny pink lips.

Lara's heart clenched. She could have had a daughter like this, if only ... no, she wouldn't go there. Not now. She let go of Abi's fingers. "Well, this room still looks the same. It definitely says ranch house with the longhorns and leather furniture. I always loved it."

Eve's smile was warm and welcoming. "It's my favorite room in the house, too. Would you like a glass of wine or iced tea?"

More at home, Lara answered, "Wine would be wonderful."

"Is chardonnay okay?"

Lara nodded, holding out her arms and hoping the baby would come to her.

With a grateful smile, Eve said, "She's heavy," and handed her over.

Abi came willingly, reaching for Lara's dangling black earrings which matched her blouse. Lara kissed the baby's cheek and snuggled her close.

Adam caught her gaze and smiled, understanding in his eyes. He knew how this baby pulled at Lara's need.

She bit her lip and bent to Abi again. "Let's find you something to play with, sweet thing." Taking her to her blanket, she set her on the floor and kneeled down beside her, handing her a toy.

Adam sat near them on the couch, tucking a wayward lock of hair behind Lara's shoulder. "You're beautiful tonight."

She turned to him and love and adoration glowed in his gaze. "Thank you. I'm glad we're here."

He squeezed her hand as Eve came back in and handed Lara her glass of wine, asking, "Is she being good for you?"

Lara ruffled the baby's soft little blonde curls. "She's a darling. You're lucky she's such a good baby."

Eve laughed. "Oh, she has her moments. But, you're right. She's an easy keeper, as her dad puts it."

Annie came in to tell them the food was ready, and Eve gathered Abi into her arms.

Lara suddenly felt empty—a bit of light going out inside her. Climbing to her feet, she followed the others to the dining room.

Over dinner, her eyes strayed to Abi with every sound the baby made. Lara watched each bite as Eve slid food into the baby's mouth and as the little one ate her finger food. Having revealed the story of her loss to Adam, her need was exposed as well.

Adam must have noticed her fixation. He slipped his arm around her shoulders and kissed her temple, whispering, "I love you. I'll never leave you."

She leaned into him, glad of the warm contact, yet unable to take her eyes from Abi. Their baby would have been dark headed and dark eyed like Adam. But she would have been just as beautiful as little Abi. Lara's heart twisted. Their daughter would be a teenager by now. Gorgeous and probably tall like her father. Lara closed her eyes against the pain, and sucked in a breath. This was no good. She took a bite of the wonderful chicken breast Annie had cooked.

After dinner, Eve took her daughter from her booster chair. "I need to get this little darling into her bath. Will you excuse me?"

"I'd be glad to help," Lara offered, imagining the tiny girl playing in the tub.

Eve smiled. "Oh, would you? Two people make bath time so much easier. Follow me."

Lara held the squirming Abi, who heard her bath running, while Eve pulled out pajamas, a tiny towel and baby toiletries.

Eve said, "You can set her here on the bed and undress her, if you don't mind."

Her fingers unsteady, Lara took off the little dress Abi wore and then removed her diaper. Picking her up, she walked in to join Eve in the bathroom.

"Go ahead and put her in the tub. I usually sit on the edge and let her play with her toys for a little while."

Abi reached for the water as Lara set her down on her bottom, making happy baby sounds and splashing loudly with her hands. She looked into Lara's eyes and laughed, splashing so hard that water wet Lara's blouse.

A tide of joy raced through Lara and she thought of Adam. Someday, maybe she'd play with her own baby in the tub. She picked up a plastic cup from the side of the bathtub and poured warm water over Abi's back.

Abi cooed and put a little boat in her mouth.

Eve said, "You've figured out what she likes. She loves it when I pour her warm bath water on her. Unless I'm washing her hair. She hates that with a passion."

A few minutes later, Eve asked to change places. "I'll wash her now so we can get back to those two men. Who knows what they're getting up to?"

Lara laughed and moved over to stand by the vanity while Eve quickly bathed her daughter and gathered her into the towel Lara handed her.

With the baby clean and dressed in her pajamas, they headed back to the family room.

Caleb and Adam sat with drinks in their hands, visiting quietly.

Lara joined Adam on the couch and he slid his arm around her shoulders. "How was bath time?"

"Glorious. Abi's such a happy baby, though I think I should have worn an apron." She pointed to the water on her blouse. "That little girl takes after her daddy. She's pretty rowdy."

Caleb laughed.

Eve brought Abi to her dad. "Give Daddy kisses goodnight, sweetheart."

He picked up his daughter and snuggled her, then kissed her neck, making her giggle. "Goodnight, sweet girl, Daddy loves you." He handed her back to Eve.

She took the baby over to Adam and Lara for kisses before carrying Abi to bed. A part of Lara's heart went with her.

When the time came to leave, Lara gave Adam's sister-in-law a hug. "I'm glad we got to spend some time with each other tonight, Eve. I hope we can be friends."

Eve smiled. "We already are. Let's get together soon for some girl time. I know your schedule must be busy, and I travel, but we can make it work."

When Adam brought Lara back to her house, she could tell he was disappointed when she said, "Do you mind if we call it an early night? I'm sorry, but I really ... I just need some time to myself tonight."

He pulled her into a gentle hug. "I understand. I'll call you tomorrow."

She leaned back and drew his face down for a soft, lingering kiss. "I love you, Adam."

He smiled and kissed her forehead. "I love you, too, sweetheart."

Locking the door behind him, her sense of aloneness returned. She needed to face the roiling emotions that Abi had brought into the light. Heading back to the bedroom, Lara shed her clothes and crawled naked into bed. Talking about her lost baby had been hard, but holding the little blonde-haired Abi and bathing her, had affected Lara on a visceral level—made her loss palpable in a way that speaking about it hadn't. The pain of losing her daughter hadn't been this bad in years.

Though Adam would have gladly held her in his arms as she worked her way through her heartache, a part of her wasn't yet ready to completely bare her grief. Pulling a pillow against her belly, she closed her eyes, giving in to her sorrow. She had no tears to pay homage to it, only a soul-deep pain. Yes, someday she may have another child, but this, her first baby, had been relegated to the dark recesses of her mind for far too long. Her little girl hadn't been well mourned. Lara had forced her daughter and her memory into oblivion years ago. It was time to rectify that.

Chapter Nine

EARLY THE NEXT MORNING, after a night of little sleep, Lara left a message for her assistant that she shouldn't expect Lara in at all. Carrying a plastic shoebox, she made her coffee strong and settled in the soft, overstuffed chair in the living room, her feet tucked under her. Covering her legs with a bright lap quilt her mother had made when Lara went away to college, she sipped the hot liquid, feeling it slide down her raw throat and hit her belly like a brand.

In the end, her mourning had found tears of release last night. At her lowest, deep, gut-wrenching sobs had nearly torn her in two. An abiding sadness still blanketed her.

She opened the shoe box which was stuffed tight with pictures. Her roommate in college that first year had taken a photography class and Lara had been one of her favorite subjects. Picking through the photos, she found one of herself sitting on a bench without a care in the world. Her heart ached for the innocent happiness in that young Lara's eyes. She kept looking and finally found the picture she sought. She stood smiling, four months pregnant, in front of a beautiful green topiary on campus, her hand caressing her belly bump.

She peered at it. Her fingers tightened on the photo, wetness pooling in her eyes. This was the last taken of her child. She drew the picture to her lips, then placed it on the side table, picking through the photos again. Sifting through more and more pictures, she couldn't find it. Dumping the box upside down on the floor, she got on her hands and knees, turning each photo over and looking at it.

Finally, she found it. Heaving a sigh, she clasped her baby's picture—the sonogram that had shown her that she was having a little girl. Her hand trembled as she brought it in for a closer look. Though she knew it was pointless with the upcoming adoption, she had named her baby Ellie, short for Elizabeth. Ellie's ribs showed clearly in the picture and she had a perky little nose. Lara traced her finger over her baby, imagining her soft skin and smelling her sweet baby scent. With a kiss, she set the photo next to the other on the table and gathered the rest, putting them back in the box.

Later, after the stores opened, she went into town and bought a baby photo frame that would accommodate both pictures. It was pink and white and made for a baby girl. Lara spent the next half hour at home framing them.

When she finished, she made another cup of coffee and set the frame beside her chair. Sitting covered with her quilt, sipping her coffee and holding her baby girl's photos in her hand, she was overcome with a sense of completion, of rightness. Ellie had existed, she'd deserved to be acknowledged, and now she was.

ADAM STRODE TO THE kitchen and opened the fridge, not really hungry, but restless. Nothing appealed to him, and he closed the door. He needed to see Lara. Seeing little Abi last night had obviously upset Lara. He had wanted to comfort her.

Instead, she shut him out, sending him home. When would she start turning to him for solace? He was here for her now—she wasn't alone.

He had today and tomorrow off. Maybe he could work something out. He texted:

What are you doing right now?

Her answer came right back:

I'm home. I took the day off.

Perfect! Now if he could entice her further.

That's great! I want you to be a very bad girl and take tomorrow off, too. Seriously, you know you haven't taken off like you should have in years. Make time now. Let's go camping this afternoon. We can hike and cook out like old times. I have a tent—the whole works. We'll come back tomorrow evening. Please, please say yes.

She wrote back:

Two days off in a row is not a good idea.

He typed:

Do you have court tomorrow?

He waited and at last she replied:

Let me call my assistant and find out what's up.

He laughed. Yes!

Awesome. I'll be right here waiting.

A few minutes later she wrote:

I'm terrible. I put off one client two days in a row and Beverly rescheduled several others. But, I'm free tomorrow.

He shoved his fist at the ceiling.

I'll pick you up in a couple of hours and bring everything we need. Be ready, girl.

He bounced to his feet and headed to the grocery store. After buying enough to eat for two days, he packed an ice chest with the food and another with the beer and wine he'd purchased and put them in the truck. Then he grabbed the camping gear from the garage and loaded it, too. From the back-yard stack, he gathered enough firewood and kindling for two fires and dumped that in the back of the truck as well. Finally, he packed his bag and drove over to Lara's house.

One thing about her hadn't changed. She was ready to walk out the door when he arrived. Besides her backpack, she had two bottles of wine and an opener in a bag. "I didn't know if you'd think of this."

He grinned. "Nice," and wrapped his arms around her, kissing her with a smack. "We're going to have a blast."

"When did you go camping last?"

"It's been a while. Gerry, a friend of mine, came to visit a couple of years ago, and we hiked the Skyline Drive Trail one day. He's not in very good shape so that was enough for him." He grinned. "You're much better company. He snored."

She laughed and picked up her bags, following him out the door.

Adam had made a reservation at the Davis Mountains State Park campground so an hour later, they were setting up their tent in a campsite that actually had some shade. Now that school was back in session, they had a great choice of sites.

He unzipped a sleeping bag and laid it on the floor of the tent, then spread two blankets on top, adding pillows to complete the bed. Wiggling his brows, he asked, "Bring back any memories?"

She cracked up. "Are we hiking today or just relaxing?"

"What do you feel like doing?"

She stared up at the mountain range. "I didn't get much sleep last night. How about we hang out this evening and hike tomorrow?"

It was nearing three already. "I like it. Let me put the chairs in the shade of that oak tree, and we'll kick back. Would you like some of the wine you brought?"

"Oh, yeah."

He set the chairs side-by-side, arms touching so he could hold her hand, and then opened one of the bottles he had chilling in the ice chest. Though it was fall, it was in the low eighties today, and the chilled wine would taste good. He twisted the cap off his beer and sat down beside Lara, handing her a glass of wine. "Relax and enjoy, my love."

Her lips quirked up. She looked off into the distance.

Her eyes were bloodshot. She must have cried a lot last night along with losing sleep. Dammit, he should have been with her. He reached for her hand. "I love you."

She glanced down at their hands, then up at him. "I love you, too. Thanks for this. I needed to get away." Looking off, she was quiet for a moment. "I have something to show you." She went to the truck and dug in her pack, coming back with a rectangular white object held to her chest with both hands.

She sat down, still clasping it close. A few seconds later she extended her hand, holding a child's photo frame with two photos. She passed it to him. "This is our daughter. It's all I have."

An electric shock slammed him. His baby? How? He tossed his beer away and grabbed the frame. Immediately he realized one was a sonogram. A warm wave swooshed through him at the first sight of her tiny head and arms and legs. The stark black-and-white photo's detail was grainy, yet he couldn't take his eyes from it—memorizing every bit of her little body. Next, he moved to the picture of Lara—her belly swollen with his child, looking so happy and innocent. God! He should have been there beside her! Wetness formed in his eyes and his lip trembled. "Lara, I'm so sorry. How did you bear it?"

She shook her head. "I don't know."

He clenched the white frame with the pink ceramic bow. "How can you forgive me?"

She freed his hand and clasped it. "I do forgive you. We were young. We both made mistakes. I framed these photos today, and I'm keeping them at my bedside. I called her Ellie, for Elizabeth."

He looked at her picture again, running his fingertip over it. "Our little Ellie."

Gripping his knee, she said, "We won't forget her. Never again. She lived inside me, and maybe it was only for a little while. But she lived."

Adam laid the frame on his lap and pulled Lara into his arms, kissing her gently, cupping her head in his hand and making her mouth, her heart, his. "We'll never forget our Ellie." When he released Lara, she seemed at peace.

He slid his arm around her shoulders and leaned back in his chair, drinking in his surroundings, loving that they shared their baby now. The trilling whistles of a Grace's Warbler, a bird common in the park, came from the limbs above them. A slight breeze carried the sharp scent of the juniper tree near the picnic table. Closing his eyes, he was content in a way he hadn't been in so long he couldn't remember.

In a little while, he stood and refilled Lara's glass and got another beer from the ice chest. "The ranger warned me about the javelinas. Said they'd been coming into the campsites a lot this year. Remind me to keep the ice chest in the truck tonight."

She grimaced. "Yeah, and the tent zipped. Ugh. I don't want those tusks anywhere near me."

He was licensed to carry and had his Walther handgun with him. Using it was the last thing he wanted to do, but he would before he let anything hurt Lara. "I'm sure we'll be okay, but I'll bring my gun in the tent."

She patted his arm, sending a warm flush through his chest.

He asked, "You getting hungry?" It was almost five.

"I probably could eat by the time we get dinner cooked."

Drinking the last of his beer, he said, "We're having hamburgers. It won't take long to get everything ready." He stood and pulled her into his arms. His hands traced the contours of her body as his mouth caressed hers. His kiss, gentle and sweet, bared his soul.

She snuggled against him.

He patted her butt, smiling, and moved to the truck to get out the propane stove for dinner. While he cooked the patties, Lara prepared the fixings, and it wasn't long before they were sitting at the table enjoying their meal. He grinned at her, his mouth full. "Just like old times."

Lara licked mayonnaise from the corner of her mouth. "Yeah, baby."

He laughed and bumped her with his shoulder.

When they finished eating, there was only the skillet and some silverware to wash. He took care of it while Lara put everything away. As he dried the pan, he asked, "Want to take a walk before it gets dark?"

She patted her belly. "Sure, I need to work this off before it turns to fat."

"*Pft*. Not a chance. We'll just walk here around the campgrounds, though. Take it easy."

A few minutes later, hand in hand, they set off. Passing other campsites, some occupied, some not, they headed for Keesey Creek, one of the few water sources in the surrounding areas. Once off the road, they watched carefully for snakes. Adam leading the way, they wound around cactus and catclaw acacia bushes in the tall, sparse grass to find a place to sit under the shady oaks lining the stream. They took off their shoes and let the quick-running water cool their feet.

He snugged Lara against him, scoring the creek side with a stick. "I don't have a care in the world right now." Kissing the side of her head, he wanted the day to go on forever. The gurgling sound of the flowing water, the splash as it hit the stones, the birds calling in the trees overhead—it all wove a magical spell that he never wanted to break.

Sighing, she clasped his hand at her waist. "I feel it, too." She closed her eyes. "This is so peaceful I could fall asleep right here."

He squeezed her. "Sleeping beauty in the forest of trees."

She grinned. "Hardly," and yawned. "Too bad it's too late for a nap, though. I haven't been this relaxed in ages."

Imagining her sleeping form in the tent, a ripple of excitement ran through him. With moonlight shining through the fabric walls, he'd make love to this amazing woman. Kissing her again, he said, "You may need that catnap. I want you strong for tonight, woman."

She laughed and elbowed him in the ribs.

Just before dusk, they put their shoes on and wound their way through the grass back to the road, heading to camp. He set about making a fire in the ring provided while Lara got him a beer and poured herself a glass of wine.

By the time darkness fell, the fire had quit smoking and Adam moved their chairs near the bright orange and yellow flames. He reached for her hand. "I love being able to see the stars at night. Remember when we used to go to Marfa and look for UFOs?"

She nodded, smiling. "I was always so sure that we'd see one. We'd stare at the sky for hours."

His heart ached for the innocence of those times. If he'd only known what lay ahead of them. He would never have left Lara's side. "We've always liked so many of the same things. You were my best friend. Not the guys I hung with."

Looking into his eyes, she said, "You were mine, too. It hurt so badly to lose you, Adam."

He slid his arm around her, pulling her close and resting his cheek against her. "I can't say sorry enough, Lara. You can trust me never to leave you again." He held her like that, willing the truth to make its way to her heart.

When she drew back, he released her. She sipped her wine, looking into the flames, the glow casting warm shadows across her face.

They spoke quietly about old things and new as the fire gradually burned down. When only coals remained, he said, "Let's go to bed."

She turned to him and nodded.

He used the dish tub and poured water on the embers as Lara brushed her teeth and washed her face by the light of the electric lantern. After doing the same, he joined her in the tent. Taking the side of the sleeping bag by the door, he pulled off his t-shirt and slid out of his shorts and briefs.

Lara laughed. "Like I said, you love being naked."

Grinning, he said, "Your turn," and went for the hem of her shirt.

She giggled and got there first, yanking her t-shirt over her head. Turning her back to him, she said, "My bra, if you please."

"My pleasure, madam." Damn, he was already hard as he anticipated seeing her beautiful body without clothes. Quickly unhooking her bra, he slid it off her shoulders.

She tossed it at the foot of the sleeping bag and slipped out of her jeans and panties.

Shit, she was gorgeous.

Turning on her side, she grinned at him. "This is a familiar scenario, mister."

He opened a condom and put it on, then pulled her over on top of him. "It surely is, ma'am." Her skin was silky smooth as he ran his hand over her butt. It was smaller than before, but still curvy. Raising her to a sitting position, he cupped her full breasts, loving the heaviness of them in his hands. As he rubbed his thumbs across her taut nipples, she hissed a breath. He pulled her ass higher on his chest and drew her breast into his mouth, flicking her nipple with his tongue.

She ground her hips against him, her head thrown back.

His tongue circling, sucking, he drew a gasp from her. He moved to her other breast, drawing it inside his mouth, massaging her nipple until she cried out, her hips writhing. He shoved her back so that she rode his cock, but he wasn't inside her—not yet. He pulled her forward and rocked her back, the sensation exquisite.

Eyes closed, she clasped his hands, canting her pelvis so that his cock hit her sensitive places. God, she turned him on. He sat up and kissed her hard.

Eyes open now, she thrust inside his mouth, fucking him with her tongue.

He moaned and laid back, lifting her high and setting his head at her opening.

She looked into his eyes and lowered herself down, taking all of him.

Clasping her butt, he closed his eyes and groaned. She felt so tight, so good. He couldn't move or he'd come. She started to rock and he held her still. "Give me a sec, babe." Taking a deep breath, he silently talked himself down from the brink. He pulled her forward again. The light of a three-quarter moon came through his tent, outlining her with its pale glow.

She leaned down and kissed him, holding his face in her hands, whispering, "I love you, my sweet Adam. I'm so glad I found you again."

His heart sped up as his love for her rushed through him. It filled him with overwhelming emotions, such joy, he couldn't hold it in. He pulled her to his chest, wrapping his arms around her as tears leaked from his eyes. "My God, I love you, Lara. I ... you're everything I want, everything I need. I don't have the words to tell you how I feel. I just ... love you, Lara."

She smiled and clasped his hands, sitting up and rocking back and forth again.

He raised her up, and pulled out of her, then slid in and pulled out, faster and faster until his hips slammed against her.

Closing her eyes, her long curls bounced with each thrust.

He stopped before he exploded, panting and wanting to make her scream with need. He flipped her on her back and slid a pillow under her hips.

She looked at him, smiling, her eyes dark with desire.

Opening her thighs, he moved between them, lowering his mouth to her curls. She was wet and the smell of her arousal nearly made him come. Spreading her, he stroked her with his tongue, finding her sensitive nub and caressing it until she cried his name.

Her hands clenched him, she arched her back, yet still he teased and worked her folds. She tossed her head, canting her hips. His mouth never stopped working her wet center.

Suddenly, she jerked, fluid gushed, and she spasmed around him, crying, "Adam, please!" as she pulled at him.

Sliding her legs over his shoulders, he rose, thrusting deep inside her. Sound ricocheted off the tent walls as his hips pounded against hers. Her little pants at each of his thrusts drove him wild. The need to explode built in him, a rising crescendo. His pulsing cock raced to climax. He thundered into her a last time, pouring his seed into the sheath encircling him, wishing he didn't have to wear it. Wishing he could start a new baby with the woman he loved.

THE NEXT DAY, HE GLANCED across at Lara as he drove home. She looked happy but exhausted. He smiled, "Are you sore?"

She grimaced. "Yes, dammit. I hate being this out of shape. I can remember taking the Skyline Drive Trail to the overlook and back and never breaking a sweat. I'm wiped out."

He grinned. "Just means we need to do this more often."

She nodded. "I had fun. I haven't been camping since the last time you and I went. I'd forgotten how much I love it."

"I do, too." He reached for her hand. "Let's plan another trip soon." He had laid awake long into the night, thinking of something else. This trip had brought them closer, but Lara still held part of herself in reserve. He would give anything, do anything, to marry her. For that to happen, he needed her to banish all her demons. To give herself fully to him as he gave him-self to her. He prayed she could find a way to do that.

Chapter Ten

LARA STOMPED HER FOOT down into her new boots. Knowing that horseback riding wasn't in her future, she'd bought city-girl western boots. The comfortable square-toes were in fashion, but what she loved most were the embroidered white and pink roses that covered the tan leather. She'd also purchased a pair of low-rise bootcut jeans and a beautifully tooled black belt with embedded-turquoise and a silver horse-shoe-shaped buckle. Her turquoise silk blouse and silver drop earrings set off her outfit perfectly. Her mass of dark curls flowing down her back pleased her as she turned and examined herself in the mirror. She hadn't dressed western since she first left Texas.

Adam was taking her country dancing tonight. Another thing she hadn't done since high school. But they'd loved dancing back then, and he was good at it. His strong arms had always guided her skillfully across the floor, and she couldn't wait to try it again.

The doorbell rang. When she answered it, a stunning Adam stood before her dressed in starched Wranglers and shirt, a grey felt cowboy hat pulled down over his eyes, and a leather belt with silver conchos and lacing at his hips.

He stepped in the door and planted a kiss on her lips first thing. "You're gorgeous. How did I get so lucky?" He grinned and grabbed her, squeezing her butt with both hands.

She laughed. "I was just thinking the same thing, cowboy." Stuffing her driver's license in her back pocket and her lipstick in her front, she was ready to go.

Adam clasped her hand as they walked to his truck. "I invited Caleb and Eve to join us. I hope you don't mind. They'll meet us there."

"Great." It would be nice to see Eve again. Having another couple to hang out with was a bonus of Adam having brothers.

Fifteen minutes later, they pulled into the parking lot of The Trail Boss Saloon. It had live music on Saturday nights and a dance floor. The only country and western place to dance in Ft. Stockton, it was always packed. Knowing this, Adam had made sure they arrived early so they could snag a table. Once Lara was seated, he went to the bar to order their drinks.

She didn't see one familiar face. It would take time to meld back into the community again.

Adam set her wine in front of her, then scooted over and put his arm across the back of her chair. "Do you still remember how to dance, girl?" He grinned, challenging her.

She fired back. "Damned straight, cowboy. You'd better not step on my toes."

He laughed and hugged her shoulders, taking a swallow of his beer. "Caleb said to save them a place. They won't be here for a while. Mom and Dad are watching Ellie, and Eve wants to get her fed, bathed and ready for bed before they head this way."

Lara envisioned that sweet routine, and felt a familiar sadness. "Makes sense. They're lucky to have your parents right there as baby sitters."

"Mom and Dad love it. They keep expecting me to settle down and produce another grandchild for them. I get regular not-so-subtle hints."

She winced and turned away. If only Roy and Millie knew that he should have had a teenager by now.

He hugged her. "Hey, there, none of that," and kissed her temple. "I love you, honey."

Nodding, she took a sip of wine. He was right. This was a night for happiness. For moving forward. How lucky she was to have the steadfast love of this wonderful man. She reached behind his neck, pulling him down for a lingering kiss, not caring who noticed.

He smiled, looking into her eyes. "I love it when you do that."

"I love you," she said, meaning every word.

The band came out on stage and started tuning their instruments and adjusting their mics. It wouldn't be long before the night began.

The place had filled up fast and a young man stopped at their table, grabbing the back of one of the empty chairs. "Are these seats taken?"

Adam said, "I'm sorry, they are. My brother and his wife are joining us."

The guy smiled and nodded and walked back to the bar.

Adam slid his arm around her shoulders, his fingers caressing her.

Sighing, a sense of belonging, of rightness, swept through her. She was finally where she was meant to be. She leaned her head against his shoulder and let the sounds of the evening wash over her—glasses clinking, muffled voices and laughter, picked guitar strings, and random keyboard riffs. She was here with the man she loved, and the whole night in his arms lay ahead of her. Smiling, she closed her eyes, happy way down to her toes.

A waitress brought drinks to the band and they joked and laughed with her for a few minutes. The drummer beat a quick riff and took a swallow from his glass. The waitress left and shortly after the music began as they played their version of Garth Brooks' song, *Friends in Low Places*.

Adam squeezed her arm gently. "Dance with me?"

She stood, butterflies in her stomach. Surely this was like riding a bike.

He led her to the floor. Clasping her waist and her hand, he pulled her against him and swung her into the first step.

His rhythm was perfect. The two-step came back to her as if her last dance was yesterday. She leaned into him and relaxed as he guided her across the dance floor, twirling and striding to the beat of the music. She closed her eyes, his arms and hands telling her feet exactly where to step. She gave her body over to him—let him have total control. It was perfect—like magic. When the song ended and she opened her eyes, she smiled up at him. "I trust you, Adam, with everything I am."

He drew her into his chest and squeezed the breath out of her, holding her there as the other couples left the dance floor. At last, it was only them, and he drew back. "Thank you, Lara. I promise, you won't regret it." Wrapping his arm around her, he brought her to the table.

As the band played the next song, she sipped her drink, hyper-sensitive to the touch of Adam's fingertips on her arm. He leaned in to speak in her ear and his breath moved a strand of her hair, sending tingles straight through her. Sliding her hand to his thigh, she caressed him, loving him so much in that moment that she wanted to kiss him hard, in front of everyone. She bit back a grin and took a sip of wine. *Down, girl.*

Adam kissed her cheek, sending goosebumps down her chest, tightening her nipples. *This silk blouse will show everything.* She turned her face to him, spotting Eve and Caleb heading toward them, and waved them over.

Caleb held a chair for Eve. "Hey, you all, sorry we're late."

"No problem, the music just started," Adam said.

Eve gave Lara a hug. "It's great to see you. I'm looking forward to this. We haven't been out in forever."

Lara grinned. "Having you all with us will make tonight a lot more fun."

Caleb left to get their drinks as Adam asked, "How is my adorable niece?"

Eve rolled her eyes. "Feisty. That's what took so long. She didn't cooperate with a single thing. I think she knew we were leaving her."

The next song started, a cowboy waltz, and Adam drew Lara to her feet. On the dance floor, he pulled her in close, and they glided away, swirling and swaying to the music. He was a wonderful, expressive dancer, and she felt every movement of his tall, muscular body against hers. Too soon, the song was over and he kissed her cheek, releasing her.

Back at the table, Adam ordered her another glass of wine and himself a beer.

Caleb and Eve had also danced. Caleb held Eve's chair for her as she said, "Whew, it's been a while since we've been on a dance floor. Thank God I didn't step on his toes."

Lara laughed. "I was worried, too. Adam's such a great dancer, though, I don't have a chance to misstep." She turned to him and smiled.

He nodded, tipping his hat.

Having to nearly shout over the music, for the next couple of songs Caleb talked about a problem he was having with one of the bulls.

Then they all danced again. She watched Caleb and Eve out of the corner of her eye. Eve wasn't short, but Caleb's tall frame would make any woman look tiny. He would have dragged his wife all over the dance floor if he hadn't shortened the steps he took with those long legs of his. They were a beautiful couple and men and women alike turned to look at them as they danced by.

Lara and Eve had to yell to be heard but managed to get in some girl talk while the guys spoke about the ranch. After a few more dances, Eve motioned to Lara before she could sit down, and they headed for the ladies' room.

After finishing in the stalls, they both put on more lipstick. Eve looked over at Lara and said, "I've never seen Adam this happy. He practically glows."

Eve's words sent a warm wave rippling through Lara. She met Eve's gaze in the mirror. "He's a good man. I'm lucky he cares for me."

Eve put her arm around Lara as they walked out the door and said, "I'm ready for another glass of wine."

A little while later the waitress stopped by and asked Adam if he wanted another beer. "Nothing for me. Lara, would you like more wine?"

She covered her glass. "No thanks." When the waitress walked away, Lara turned to Adam, "I'm already getting tired. Any more wine and I'll fall asleep on you."

He scooted his chair a couple of inches closer. "Come here, babe." Wrapping his arm around her, he snuggled her against him and kissed her cheek.

She lifted her face, inviting his kiss.

With infinite gentleness, he brushed her lips with his, and said, "I love you, darling."

Tucking her face into his chest, knowing that her heart, her life, was safe with him—she let herself trust Adam completely.

THE NEXT MORNING, ADAM listened to the chest of a very sick little boy. It being Sunday, his parents didn't feel they should wait another day for a visit to their pediatrician. Little Blake had a fever of 105 degrees and a terrible cough. Tossing his stethoscope over his head, Adam made some notes on Blake's chart and ordered the necessary tests.

His mother asked, "What do you think is wrong with him?"

Adam looked up. "I think we've caught it in time. He doesn't appear to have pneumonia though X-rays will give me a better look. We'll also take some blood work. I'll start him on antibiotics and something for his cough and fever and someone will be down to give him a breathing treatment in a little while."

She ran her fingers through Blake's hair. "Thank goodness. We were so worried when his fever climbed so high."

Adam smiled as he turned to go. "We'll fix him up before we send him home. He'll be just fine."

Adam handed Blake's chart to the nurse and opened the door, his mind already on Lara again. When he took her home last night, she'd drawn him straight to the bedroom, kissing him passionately and unbuttoning his shirt as she said, "I love you, Adam. I want to make love to you and show you just how much." And she had. Her desire for him had been so exciting, so erotic, he'd been hard put to last until she could come with him.

At the bar, when she'd said she truly trusted him, he knew, at last, they had a foundation that a loving marriage could rest on. And, with her lovemaking last night, she knew it, too. Starting today, they could build a relationship based on trust and friendship. One he hoped would lead to marriage in the not-too-distant future.

He sat at his desk in the center of the ER and sent a quick text:

Missing you terribly. Hope you slept in. Loved last night and love you.

She texted back:

Miss you, too. Wish you didn't have to work today. I'm sure you're tired. Love you.

He grinned and picked up the next patient's chart, imagining the kiss he'd give her when he saw her after work. Life didn't get any better than this.

LARA FLIPPED ON HER Mercedes' blinker, slowing down to turn into Adam's subdivision. The past two weeks had flown by. She and Adam had grown as close as they had ever been. Spending almost every night together, either at her home or his, she'd come to depend on having his arms wrapped around her when she fell asleep. He was cooking tonight, and she looked forward to drinking wine and visiting with him while he walked back and forth in his manly apron.

Parking in his driveway, she gathered her bag and purse and headed for his door, wishing the weather were better. She should hire a yardman. She compared her yard to Adam's. His place was always so perfectly groomed, and she was consistently behind.

Adam answered the door and gave her a hug. "Dinner's cooking, come on in."

She followed him to the kitchen and sat at the bar as he poured her a glass of sauvignon blanc. "It smells fabulous in here, Adam. It's what? Oregano and garlic? Maybe thyme? Tell me what we're having."

"Greek chicken breasts and a Greek salad and, following the theme, coconut lime dessert made with Greek yogurt."

"You're amazing. I can't wait to eat." The narrow bib of the apron accentuated his broad chest. Little ripples of desire raced up her belly. He was her man, and she couldn't get enough of him. "I see you've started the salad." She dipped her nose in the bowl, smelling the oregano-covered tomato wedges and sliced onions. "Yum. I'm starving."

Adam stood at the stove, browning the chicken breasts. "I marinated these overnight in the fridge. I love Greek food. I wish Ft. Stockton had a Greek restaurant."

A warm, delicious feeling filled her. He looked so domestic, standing there in his apron, holding the handle of the skillet and turning the meat. She imagined him, ages from now, as her husband, still caring for her. Sipping her wine, she accepted that a future like this could be hers.

Adam forked the chicken breasts on a small platter and put them on the dining room table. They were eating inside tonight because of the weather. Rain was on the way and wind blew fiercely outside. He returned to the fridge and pulled out a bag of cucumbers, bell pepper, olives and feta cheese, dumping it into the salad bowl. Stirring everything together, he liberally added olive oil.

After setting the salad on the table beside the chicken, he took off his apron and refilled their wine glasses. "Let's eat. I'm starving, too."

The rich aroma coming from the food made her mouth water. "How did you become such a good cook?"

He grinned. "The internet, babe. Isn't that what everyone does nowadays?"

She served salad on her plate. "I can't wait to try this, and it looks so simple to make."

"I only do simple."

After forking a piece of chicken and setting it next to her salad, she handed the platter to Adam. "I'm finding it harder and harder to keep up with your prowess in the kitchen."

He raised his brows. "So, it's a competition? I'll have to remember that and study more."

She grinned. "Cut me some slack. I'm not used to this whole cooking thing yet." Sipping her wine, which was wonderful with the savory scent of the food, she relaxed into the back of her chair. As hungry as she was, it was fabulous to sit here and enjoy the effortless experience of dinner with her lover.

Adam stopped chewing and looked at her. "So, how is it?"

"Give me a minute." She cut a piece of chicken and popped it in her mouth, letting the spices swirl together as she slowly chewed. "It's fantastic, Adam. I need this recipe."

He smiled and resumed eating. "I guess I can give my secret away. It's on the counter in the kitchen."

The salad was just as amazing as it smelled. She speared a wedge of ripe tomato covered in salt and oregano and moaned when she chewed it. "Adam, I'm in heaven. This is to die for."

"I told you we'd do goodfood tonight." He grinned and took another bite of chicken.

After dinner, she helped him clean up and they headed to the living room to relax. She'd just snuggled into his chest with her glass of wine when the doorbell rang.

He frowned.

"You expecting anybody?"

"No, I seldom have company."

She could see the front door from her seat on the couch.

When Adam answered it, a tall, beautiful blonde in a long rain coat brushed past him and walked into the house.

Adam turned, following her. "I told you how it stood between us. Please leave," he said sharply.

Confused, Lara peered at the blonde's face.

Ignoring him, the woman caught sight of Lara and walked briskly into the living room. "Hello, I'm Demi. I tried calling Adam but couldn't reach him."

Lara bit her lip. Why was this beautiful woman here, and why had she been trying to call Adam?

Adam said loudly, "That's because I—"

The blonde interrupted him. "I really wanted to see him tonight so I thought I'd come by. He loves it when we have sleepovers."

Lara jerked her head back. Sleepovers? What the hell?

Adam lurched toward the woman. "Dammit, Demi! Shut the fuck up!"

Before he could get to her, she unbelted her coat and threw it open, exposing the fact that she wore only a tiny black lace bra and panties and a garter belt holding up sheer black hose. She took a step toward Lara. "He likes it when I wear this, too."

Adam grabbed her and growled, "You're a bitch for trying a stunt like this."

Yanking on her arm, she protested, "Let go! Don't you love me anymore? You know you want me, Adam."

"I never loved you, and you damn well know that."

He marched her to the door as she struggled against him and shoved her outside, locking it behind her.

Lara was on her feet, faint from shock.

He came to her—tried to take her in his arms.

She drew back. "Adam, I need to go."

"Lara, I'm not seeing her."

"She doesn't seem to know that." Her pulse so loud in her ears she could count the beats of her heart, she strode toward the door.

He took hold of her arm.

She looked at his hand. "Adam, please."

His eyes imploring, he said, "We need to talk about this."

"Not now. I need to think. I have to go."

Desperate, he said, "It's not what it looks like. I've done nothing to betray you. Please, believe me." He released her and stepped back.

She walked to the door. Her trust, so new and tender, had departed with the woman in the lace bra and panties.

Chapter Eleven

ADAM WATCHED, STUNNED, as Lara closed the door. The fact that she trusted him so little hurt beyond words. He thought they were past something like this. He made himself a whiskey, wanting a buffer against the grief that was fast filling his heart. Once Lara had time to think about what she knew of him, she'd realize that he wouldn't have been sleeping with another woman. That's not who he was. It never had been.

He collapsed on the sofa, overcome with dread. What if she didn't believe him? What if she didn't trust that he was true to her? He couldn't lose her. Not now. He wanted to text her but she was still driving. The thought of her believing anything that bitch Demi had said cut like a knife. Lara had said she wanted time to think, but what would she be thinking? She needed to hear the truth. But how could that happen if she wouldn't speak with him?

Lurching to his feet, he paced the room. There had to be a way to fix this. They loved each other. He gulped several swallows of whiskey. He needed to give her room—she'd asked for it—but then they were going to talk. When the truth came out, surely then, she would trust him again.

LARA DROVE HOME ON automatic, numbness creeping over her. Visions of the woman, Demi, in all her tawdry nearly-naked beauty kept flashing before her. Adam was a man, of course he would be attracted to a woman like that. She grimaced. What did she know of men, though? She could count the guys she'd dated on one hand and still have fingers to spare.

The woman had expected a warm welcome. Why? Laura rubbed her forehead, her gut leaden. It was all too confusing. What did she really know about Adam? Thirteen years ago, she'd known an innocent boy from an isolated ranch in Texas. That boy had traveled, had time to develop different tastes—different expectations of women. Did he show one kind of man to her and different wants and needs to his other lover? She shivered, the thought too horrible to think about. She loved him—had trusted him. Could he do that to her?

Back at home, she was too upset for bed, instead she poured a glass of wine and headed to the back porch. After first checking for snakes, she turned off the light and sat in the dark, her thoughts racing. This whole thing felt surreal. How could her life have changed so quickly? The only other time in her life she'd known true joy was her senior year when she and Adam were so in love. Look how that ended. Why should this time be any different?

She sipped her wine, the hollowness his loss left her with growing worse by the second. What could he say to her now, anyway? The woman didn't just show up out of the blue. And she obviously expected something of Adam. There must be a reason for those expectations.

Lara rubbed her temples. A headache throbbed, and she seldom got headaches. Her teeth clenched and she relaxed her jaws. Crap. She was a mess. She headed in to run a hot bath. While the water ran, she took something for the headache and topped off her wine. If only she could stop her whirling thoughts. Undressing quickly, she clipped her hair on top of her head.

Just before she got in the bath, a text came in. Grabbing her phone, she stepped into the steaming hot water, sighing in pleasure as she slid down in the tub, the water coming up to her neck. At the touch of a button, she saw the text was from Adam. Her stomach twisted and she laid the phone on the edge of the tub. Reading that message was the last thing she needed to do. Wetting a washcloth and covering her face with it, the heat seeped into her pores.

Still ignoring Adam's message, she opened her eyes, removing the cloth and sinking even lower until only her nose was above the water line. The intense heat baked her, relaxed her, dulled her mind. She blew bubbles, thinking of nothing and no one. Wiggling her toes, she imagined her feet buried in the sand at the beach. She needed to make a weekend getaway down to Padre Island. Leave Adam and this shithole of a mess behind. The more she thought about it, the more an escape appealed to her.

Her dad had always insisted on carrying a day planner. One of the changes she'd recently implemented was making the office calendar electronic. Now she could check her scheduled appointments from her phone at any time. Since she tried not to schedule anything on Fridays, she was free tomorrow, but scrolled through to Monday. She only had one meeting that day. She fired off an e-mail to Beverly; by morning her calendar would be clear. Next, she looked for a place to stay on the island and, twenty minutes later, had booked a condo on the beach. In no time, she found a flight from El Paso to Corpus. After scheduling a car rental, fleeing was a reality.

Euphoria filled her. It was an incredible relief to escape the loss and dread that meeting Demi had caused.

The bath water had turned cool so she washed and got out. Taking the last of her wine to the bedroom, she climbed in bed and opened her phone, reading what Adam had to say:

> *Lara, sweetheart, I'm so sorry you had to witness that mess tonight. I understand you don't want to talk about it, but I promise you, I am not seeing this woman. Please, believe in me. I love you, honey. Adam*

She wanted to believe him, desperately. But that woman was so sure of herself—had been confident Adam would welcome her. It was too confusing. Too hard.

> *I haven't stopped loving you, Adam. I'm going away. To think. Please, let me have this time alone. Lara*

Setting her phone on silent, she turned off the light and lay on her side, a pillow clutched to her belly. Her euphoria had vanished. Was this how it would be again? The thought of returning to how she lived before Adam was too much to face. Instead, she thought of the beach, slow waves rolling in, the sound of seagulls, and curling her toes in the sand.

THE FOLLOWING MORNING, Lara got up early and packed for the trip. It was a long drive to El Paso. Always one to get ready fast, she was on the road before long. After stopping for a fast-food breakfast, she merged on IH-10 and set her cruise control. Her mind, now with nothing to do, returned to the night before. She flipped on the radio, found a rock station, and cranked up the volume in hopes of a distraction.

She'd told her mother the name of the condos where she was staying, but she didn't expect to be bothered. Her mother and Beverly were to contact her only in case of an emergency.

Her arrival at the island should allow her to check in and still spend the late afternoon at the beach. She'd stop and buy a beach towel, sunscreen and a hat when she left the airport. Would North Padre have changed much? This time of year, the beach shouldn't be as crowded as when school was out for the summer. Her stomach clenched. It would have been so wonderful to share this weekend with Adam.

She unscrewed the cap from her water bottle and took a long drink. Another distraction. She refused to torture herself with thoughts of Adam or that woman.

Arriving at the airport with time to spare, she paced, waiting to board her flight. Driving and keeping her thoughts free from the tangle of uncertainty she felt had mentally worn her out, yet physically she was wired.

As one of the first to arrive, she held a good boarding pass and sat in the front of the plane when she boarded. After a stop in San Antonio, they flew into Corpus Christi, where she debarked and picked up her rental. Stopping first along the way for her purchases, she soon crossed the long bridge over the Intracoastal Waterway. Following her phone GPS, she arrived at a row of tall condo buildings scattered along the coast line. When she entered her home for the weekend, she was ready for a glass of wine and a long, relaxing time at the water.

Not even bothering to unpack, she donned her swimsuit and, with her drink and towel in hand, headed to the beach.

Few people were around. An older couple sat in chairs on the right a short way from her. To the left, a younger couple walked hand-in-hand. Dropping her towel, she waded in the water until the waves tickled her calves. Looking far out to sea she let the waves break over her. She closed her eyes, hearing the sound of the water washing up on shore, seagulls in the distance, and the wind that blew off the ocean rushing past her ears. Wiggling her toes, she let her feet sink deeper in the sand. The water, warm from the sun, ran one way and then the other across her legs. Sighing, some of the tension from the past twenty-four hours flowed from her with each breath. She needed this.

Opening her eyes, she spotted a tanker at the horizon, creeping along toward port. An oil derrick was out there, too. She clipped her hair on top of her head. Wading into deeper water, she knelt on her knees. Wave after wave massaged her tired muscles as they passed by. An occasional piece of seaweed made its scratchy way across her belly or thigh. She settled into a trancelike state—no thoughts, feeling nothing. Her breathing slowed and her muscles let go of the tension that tightened them.

After a time, at peace and relaxed, she returned to the sand and lay on her towel, letting the sun seep deep into her body. Closing her eyes, the sound of the waves lulled her. This was what she came for.

A dog barked. Her eyes flew open and she turned her head toward the sound. She must have fallen asleep. Squinting her eyes at the bright rays of the sun, she examined the woman who threw a Frisbee to the black lab that had barked. She laughed as the dog chased his toy out into the water, swimming to retrieve it.

The young woman turned to Lara and smiled. "Hi. Sorry Jasper woke you up. He gets excited when I throw his Frisbee." She came closer. "I'm Tina, by the way. You here for long?"

"Just a couple of days. You?" Lara said.

"I live around here. We come down to the water on my days off. I'm a nurse at a hospital in Corpus Christi."

Lara rose to her elbows. "I'm Lara. Sounds like you have a lot of fun."

Tina came over and sat beside her. "I love living here." She grinned. "So does Jasper." She called to her dog, who had wandered up the beach a ways, then looked back at Lara. "Are you here with someone or did you come alone?"

Lara's smile fell away. "I'm here by myself. I needed a break to think, you know?"

Tina studied her. "I understand. The ocean's a great place for that. Listen, if you want to hang tonight, give me a call." She reached for her phone which she wore in an armband. "Tell me your number, and I'll text you mine."

After a moment's hesitation, Lara rattled off her number. Why not blow off some steam, and Tina seemed like fun.

Tina stuck her phone back on her arm and got up, dusting off her butt. "Call me, girl. Jasper wants to go, so I'll see you." She grinned and jogged to catch up with her dog.

Lara stood and grabbed her towel, ready to head back and shower. Her stomach rumbled—her hurried breakfast early that morning was the only food she'd eaten all day. Tina might want to eat dinner before they found someplace to have fun.

After a warm relaxing shower and changing into comfortable clothes, she sent Tina a text about dinner. A few minutes later, her new friend replied:

> *Dinner sounds great. Let's go to the Black Marlin. How about I meet you at eight-thirty?*

Lara's stomach grumbled again at the idea of food.

> *I'll see you there.*

Thank goodness she bought some snacks earlier. After inhaling a handful of chips, she headed in to get ready.

LARA ARRIVED AT THE Black Marlin few minutes early, but Tina was already there. She waved and Lara walked over to her table.

Tina grinned. "Hi! You're going to love this place. I hope you're hungry."

"Starving!" Lara smiled and opened the menu in front of her. Glancing up, she said, "Did Jasper pout when you left him?"

Tina rolled her eyes. "Always. I already know what I want. Their crab is to die for here and their Texas fries kick ass."

Damn that sounded delicious. How did Tina stay so slim eating like that? The beautiful blonde looked like a centerfold.

Tina drummed her fingers on the table. "Have you decided what you want yet?"

What the hell. She wouldn't worry about calories this weekend. "I'll have your suggestion."

"There's a beach volleyball game tomorrow. Come with me and we'll burn off the fat from this dinner."

Beach volleyball? Her last game was buried in ancient history. "I'll probably be terrible at it."

"Don't worry. It's not a tournament or anything. We're playing for fun."

Lara was supposed to be thinking about her problem. So far, that hadn't happened. But maybe she needed some distance from it before she considered her options. "What time and where?"

Tina explained, and a couple of minutes later the waitress came by and took their order.

Tina was funny, telling Lara crazy stories about her work at the hospital. Lara could see how she would be her patients' favorite nurse, and that she really enjoyed her job.

When they finished eating, they headed over to the 361 Bar.

The music was perfect when Lara walked in and the place looked pretty classy for a beach town.

Tina found them a place to sit by the pool table. "Do you play?"

"It's been a while, but I like it."

Tina put change in the table and racked the balls.

The waitress came and Lara called out, "What are you drinking?"

As she perused the cue sticks, Tina raised her voice and said, "Margarita on the rocks. Thanks."

Lara nodded to the Waitress. "Me too, only frozen."

After finding her own stick, Lara chalked the tip. "I hope you're not a pool shark."

Tina grinned. "I'm pretty good. Look out. Do you want to break?"

"Show me what you got, girl."

Tina took aim and the cue ball rammed into the triangle of balls. Three of them went into pockets—all solids.

Lara groaned. "You weren't kidding."

"Watch and weep, girlfriend." Tina put three more solid balls in the pockets before she missed, leaving a couple of good lays for Lara.

She put three striped balls in and then missed. Groaning in frustration, she said. "Go ahead, beat me."

Tina laughed and lined up on the last solid ball, snapping it into the pocket. She didn't have a line on the eight ball, though, and missed.

Lara suddenly thought of Adam and how much fun it would be to have him here playing pool, and her joy whooshed out of her. She took aim and sent the cue ball flying at the orange-striped ball, making it hit the pocket so hard it rocketed around a few times before it landed inside.

"Wow, girl, you meant that one," Tina said and grinned.

Lara grimaced and held back a little on the next shot, but still sent her ball into the pocket. She missed her next shot, with two balls still left on the table and leaving Tina a perfect line to the eight ball.

Tina put it in easily and asked, "Another game?"

Lara shook her head, her enthusiasm gone.

Tina sat across from her, taking a swallow of her margarita. "So, what took all the air out of your sails?"

Lara sighed. "I came to Padre Island because I need to make a decision about what's happening with a relationship I'm in. I was thinking how nice it would be if he were here and, you know, blah."

Tina nodded. "Been there. Why don't you tell me about him? This is the perfect time. They'll crank up the music when more people get here."

Lara took another sip of her margarita. She may as well talk about it. Another person's insight would be good to hear. "Okay. He's a cowboy and a surgeon, and I love him. I thought I trusted him. Then ...." She told Tina all about Demi and what she'd said, how the woman looked, and what little Adam had told Lara about her.

Tina tilted her almost empty margarita glass, sucking down the last drop and looking for the waitress. After catching her attention, Tina returned her gaze to Lara. "That's messed up. I understand why you're upset. I would be, too." She swirled ice around in her glass. "He swears he's not sleeping with her?"

Lara nodded, taking a long swallow of her drink.

"Hm." Tina gazed off across the room. Glancing back at Lara, she sucked a piece of ice into her mouth and said, "Maybe this Demi has it out for him. She could have heard he was dating someone else after he quit seeing her. Some women don't take that too well."

Lara chewed her lip. "Still, what she did was kind of psycho, don't you think?"

"For sure. Makes you wonder what he saw in a witch like her."

Lara shivered. True. Why had Adam gone out with a woman who would do something so weird? All Lara had were more questions, and only Adam could answer them. She should have let him talk.

Lara reached across the table and clasped Tina's hand. "Thanks for listening. I need to give Adam a chance to explain, I guess. I won't know how to feel, or what to do until I do."

Tina ordered them both another margarita, and they visited while the place filled with partiers. As Tina had predicted, the music blasted over the speakers and voices grew louder in competition.

When she finished her drink, Lara stood and gave Tina a hug. "I need to go home. I didn't get much sleep last night, and I'm pooped out."

Tina told her the time and place of the volleyball game. "Come play. You'll have fun."

Waving goodbye, Lara made her way to her car and drove back to the condo. Once inside, she poured herself a glass of wine, changed into a gown and settled in bed. Though she'd asked for space from Adam, she needed to talk to him. Picking up her phone, she texted:

> *I've had a little while to think. I realize I didn't give you a chance to tell me about you and Demi. Will you explain about your relationship?*

He texted right back:

There was no relationship. She told me when we first met that she didn't want kids. I told her I did and got up to leave. Instead, she wanted to see me, no strings attached. We never went on a date. We met at her place or mine. We fucked, period. I saw her for about six months before I found out you were back in town. Then I immediately told her I wouldn't see her anymore. She was upset. I reminded her that she'd agreed to no strings. She hounded me with calls and texts until I finally blocked her. I had no idea she would show up at my house, Lara.

Her heart pounded as she considered his words. Was this news better or worse than she'd feared? With trembling fingers, she typed:

Thank you for telling me. Good night.

He sent:

I love you. Demi means nothing to me and never did. I didn't live the life of a monk, but I'm a faithful man, Lara.

She texted back:

I'll think about what you said and see you sometime next week.

Laying her phone on the night stand, she took a sip of wine. He'd fucked the beautiful blonde for six months. Her gut twisted. He must have liked sex with her a lot. Knifelike fingers of jealousy clawed at her. Low self-esteem was something Lara had wrangled with since her relationship with Kingsley and his subsequent rape. The knowledge she gained tonight could take her down if she let it. With a long swallow of wine, she hardened her resolve. She wouldn't give in to self-doubt, nor would she allow the other woman to become a crack in her self-image. Whatever she decided about Adam, she would stay strong.

AFTER EATING BREAKFAST out the next morning, she drove home and dressed for the beach. With a romance novel for her beach-read, she planned a quiet day to herself rather than volleyball. After texting Tina, Lara headed out.

It being a Saturday, there were a lot more people at the water. She chose a spot and laid out her towel. Turning on her belly, propped on her elbows, she started her book. Three pages later, she couldn't remember what she'd read. Visions of Adam with Demi kept breaking into her thoughts. It was stupid. If she could believe him, then he broke up with the blonde before he ever dated Lara. What man wouldn't want to fuck a willing woman who looked like Demi? Lara knew her jealousy was ridiculous yet it filled her belly with acid.

She dug her hand in the sand, encountering the coolness down deep. There had to be a way to make peace with this thing between Adam and Demi. He said he didn't care about her. Why should Lara, then? She'd never been jealous before. Not even in high school. It was a hideous, out-of-control feeling.

Laying her book down, she rested her chin on her fist. It was time to put on her big girl panties and man up. Whether she decided to believe Adam or not, she couldn't let jealousy get the best of her. She was inclined to believe him, though. He'd done nothing to make her think he was a liar or a cheat. He wasn't one when she knew him before. Surely, he hadn't changed at his core.

Needing to move, she walked into the water, out far enough that it came to her waist, letting the waves buffet her. Small sharks often came into shore, but seldom bothered anyone. They were the least of her worries right now when she had a two-legged blonde shark to think about.

She had to get control of herself. Being jealous of a time in Adam's life before they were together was unfair. More than that, it was stupid. Letting her arms float, she enjoyed the weightlessness. The water was cooler out this deep. The sun beat down on her shoulders and the cold water felt good. Because it was fall, the days here were often cloudy or rainy. Luckily, this weekend was warm with bright sunshine.

Seagulls flew out to sea, dipping into the water and swooping back into the air. Their eager cries relaxed her, as did the waves breaking against her chest. It didn't seem Adam was to blame for what happened that night. If he was telling the truth, Demi had wanted to cause a stink. The question was, how big of a stink would Lara allow it to be?

Honestly, the whole thing came down to whether she believed what Adam had told her. Had he broken it off with Demi? That was what she had to decide. No wishy-washy deciding, either. If she determined that he told the truth, then that was that, and she had to put it all behind her.

She turned around and leaned into the waves, allowing the water to support her. As Adam filled her mind—his gentleness, his strength, the way he shared his feelings with such ease—she let the sea wash away the anxiety that had tormented her. Wave after wave moved past her. Closing her eyes, burying her toes in the sand, her arms floated beside her.

When her fingers had turned into little prunes, she returned to the sand and laid down on her towel again, and this time when she began to read, she enjoyed meeting the handsome cowboy and learning how he would woo his beautiful lover.

Later, as she walked back to her room, Tina texted her:

Want to meet up? I can't stay out late because I work tomorrow, but how about dinner?

Lara texted back:

I'd love to. Tell me where.

Tina replied:

Meet me at La Playa at seven forty-five.

Back at the condo, she showered and stood at the sliding doors to the balcony, sipping a glass of wine. The day at the water had done her a world of good. Her head was clear for the first time since Demi had walked into Adam's house. Lara's confusion, her self-doubt had faded. Her future lay ahead of her. All she had to do was figure out what that future would be.

Her room, five stories high, gave her a view far down the island. A pelican flew by so close she could see individual feathers in its wings. Tiny ships moved on the horizon, traveling toward Corpus. She'd needed this trip to gain perspective. And she had. Glancing at her watch, she headed inside to get ready for dinner.

LARA FOUND A TABLE shortly before Tina arrived at *La Playa* and Lara waved to catch her attention.

Tina strode over and sat down. "Made it."

Lara raised her brows.

"I had to clean house and run all my errands since I go back to work tomorrow. I barely had time to get ready."

"You look great." Lara sipped her iced tea and smiled. The blonde looked like she belonged on a magazine cover.

The waitress came by and they ordered.

"How are you? Did you have a better day?" Tina asked.

"I did, actually. I realized a lot of my problem was jealousy. As for the rest—I just need to figure out whether I trust Adam's word or not."

The waitress set Tina's iced tea in front of her.

"It all boils down to how well you know the man I guess, right?" Tina took a sip of tea, meeting Lara's gaze.

It did. And Lara knew Adam. She'd known him as a boy, and he'd shown her the man he'd become in the past months. That man was loving, kind, dependable and true. Just as his younger self had been. "You're right." She smiled at her new friend. "Tina, I'm so glad we met. Let's stay in touch, okay? I hope you'll come visit me in Ft. Stockton sometime."

"I'd like that. I've never been to West Texas before."

Lara grinned. "I'll take you to The Trail Boss Saloon and introduce you to a cowboy or two. I'll even teach you to dance the Cotton-Eyed Joe."

Tina thrust her hand out. "It's a date, girl."

EARLY MONDAY AFTERNOON Lara set out on the long drive from the El Paso airport to Ft. Stockton. Sunday she'd gone to the Padre Island National Seashore, a national park further down the island. She walked what seemed like forever down the beach, collecting seashells. The wind blew hard all day and she got back with her skin chapped and gritty with sand. But she also felt completely relaxed and at peace with herself. She was ready to face her life again. And talk to Adam.

Chapter Twelve

AT TEN THIRTY MONDAY morning, Adam threw his stethoscope over his head and yanked open the curtain to the next room in the ER. A three-car accident on IH-10 had every room full. He'd called in the other two surgeons along with the residents and people in critical condition still needed help. All three of the ORs were in use. He'd triaged the victims as they came in and sent the two most critical patients to surgery a few minutes earlier, but a young man, the driver of a pickup truck, also needed surgery stat.

"Dr. Govain, his blood pressure is 70/40."

Adam called a verbal order to the ER nurse. "Get blood typed and crossed stat. Run colloids wide open." He called the OR to check the progress of an on-going elective surgery and spoke to the supervising nurse. "How much longer?" His tone was more terse than he intended.

"He just finished closing. Bring up your guy. We'll clean the room as fast as we can, then you can roll him in."

Every minute counted. The man was hemorrhaging. Adam had already tapped the patient's abdomen and drained the blood. Adam needed to get in there, find the source and stop the bleeding. He turned to the nurse, "We're going to the OR."

Raising the bars on the bed, he wheeled him out of the room, taking long strides toward the elevator. The wait for the car seemed interminable. The patient's face was pale, his eyes closed. Dammit! They had to hurry!

A bell dinged as the double doors opened. The nurse pulled the bed inside, and Adam followed, pushing the button for their floor. He gritted his teeth as the elevator doors slowly shut.

When they arrived outside the OR, two techs and the nurse scrambled to clean and set up the room.

Adam started the ritual scrub, the routine action calming him, though he kept an anxious eye on his patient.

The OR nurse gave the okay to enter.

Adam's nurse from the ER wheeled the bed into the room and helped slide the patient onto the operating table.

Adam pulled on a gown. A nurse tied the strings behind his neck and opened gloves for him to slide on. His mind slowed. He breathed deeply and exhaled. He was in control now.

The anesthesiologist sedated the young man. People moved into their positions.

"Scalpel." The nurse slapped the instrument on his hand, and Adam made his first cut.

AS DUSK FELL, ADAM leaned back in a chair on the patio, drinking his whiskey and going over the long day. It had been years since his skills were challenged like they had been today and he'd loved every minute of it.

When he was in Boston, most days had been like this, and he'd reveled in the excitement, the test of his knowledge and abilities that every case brought. He took another swallow of whiskey. It had taken a three-car pileup to show him how desperately he missed working somewhere he could be his best, do his best—where he saved lives every day.

His job at this small-town hospital paled in comparison. His talent was essentially wasted here. Throwing back the last of his drink, he stripped off his shirt and dove in the pool, racing from one side to the other, arms slashing through the water, kicking hard, propelling himself on mighty lungfulls of air.

He didn't stop until his exhausted limbs trembled. Holding on to the edge of the pool, he gasped for air, his heart pounding. Was this all there was? A too-simple job? A woman who didn't believe in him? He pulled himself out of the water and dried off. Dark had fallen and he moved inside.

After a shower, he fixed a sandwich and sat at the table, eating only because he needed something in his stomach. Dissatisfaction rode him hard. He took a bite and ground it between his teeth. Why wouldn't Lara believe him? He'd never been anything but honest with her. She had no reason to doubt him. And why hadn't he heard a word from her in two days? It wasn't his fault that Demi turned out to be crazy-ass.

Taking another bite, he chewed quickly. He should get the hell out of this town. He hadn't meant to live here forever, anyway. His dad was doing fine now. There was no reason to stay. Especially not if Lara turned her back on him.

His stomach clenched and he tossed his sandwich on his plate. How could she do this to him? He loved her and she'd said she loved him. Dumping his uneaten food in the trash, he turned off the light and strode to his bedroom.

Sliding into bed in the dark, he clasped his hands behind his head. His life had gone to hell. Blowing out a breath, he tried to relax. The swim had finished exhausting his already tired muscles.

His phone sounded and he glanced at the screen. A text from Lara. Dammit, he couldn't deal with her tonight. Dropping the phone back on the nightstand, he turned over.

Thirty minutes later, he still couldn't sleep. He was too tired, and, despite his wish, part of him worried about the text. Did Lara need him? Giving up, he turned over and read it.

> *Adam, I'm back. My trip to Padre was exactly what I needed to get my head straight. First, I'm sorry I didn't listen to you—didn't let you tell me whatever you wanted to say about what happened. Second, I realized after much introspection that what bothered me most was simple jealousy. And that's just plain dumb. I have no right to be jealous of something that happened before I came on the scene. That's third. I know you didn't see this woman while you were with me. You were never that kind of boy and I refuse to believe you turned into that kind of man. I hope you'll forgive me for shutting you out. And not trusting you from the beginning. I'm so sorry. I love you, Lara*

He read her text again. She believed him now. If the situation were reversed, he would have been jealous, too. He wrote back:

> *I love you. I'm glad you believe me now. Of course, I forgive you. I missed you. Adam*

She must still be awake because she texted right back:

I miss you terribly right now. Can we see each other tomorrow night?

He grinned and wrote:

You bet. Since we're both working, come to my place and I'll order pizza.

She answered:

It's a date.

He put the phone down, his outlook totally changed. It was amazing what love could do for a man.

THE NEXT EVENING, ADAM rushed through his shower, wanting to be ready when Lara arrived. He couldn't wait to pull her into his arms and kiss that luscious mouth of hers. He'd picked up a bouquet of flowers on the way home from the hospital—her favorite yellow roses with orange tips. He also purchased a bottle of Barbera d'Alba red wine to go with the pizza. As he uncorked the wine, which had been chilling since he got home, the doorbell rang. His pulse sped up as he walked to the door.

Lara had come straight from the office. The brilliant, royal-blue power suit she wore set off her striking dark hair and grey eyes. He swept her into his arms, holding her to him in a powerful embrace.

She snuggled into him. "I missed you so much, Adam."

He pulled away so he could look at her. "Damn, I'm glad you're here. Come inside." Arm across her shoulders, he led her to the kitchen. "I bought flowers."

"They're beautiful. You remembered I love these." Her eyes sparkled as she bent to smell the blooms.

Slipping his arms around her waist from behind, he nibbled her neck, loving her scent and the way her soft hair tickled his face.

She reached up and pulled his cheek to her, kissing him. "I love you."

He whispered, "I love you, too. Would you like a glass of wine?"

"Uh-hm." She smiled, leaning against the table.

"The pizza will be here any minute." He filled their glasses and handed one to her. "Let's go outside. We should be warm enough." The evenings were finally feeling like fall though the days could still be hot.

They sat side-by-side, and he laced his fingers with hers with a sense of completeness. It was crazy how miserable he'd been less than twenty-four hours ago. "Someday we need to plan a trip to the coast together."

"The place I stayed was wonderful. I had a condo right on the beach, and it would be perfect for the two of us."

"Let's do it then." Taking a swallow of wine, he said, "I'm happy we put this nonsense behind us."

"Me, too." She grinned. "If I remember correctly, our make-up sex is fabulous."

He roared a laugh and pulled her in for a kiss. "You remember right, my love."

The doorbell rang. Still grinning, he got up to answer the door. After tipping the delivery boy, he brought out the pizza, plates and napkins. Topping off their glasses, he said, "I'm hungry, how about you?"

"Starving," and she licked her lips seductively.

He laughed and sat down. "Just keep it up. You're in trouble, darling."

Grinning mischievously, she picked up a piece of pizza and took a big bite, moaning over it.

Laughing again, he grabbed a slice of his own. Damn she was fucking hot. Just watching her chew was making him hard.

The wine went perfectly with the pizza, really setting off the flavors of the cheese and tomato sauce. He took a swallow and then another bite from his slice, enjoying the hell out of the food and having his gorgeous woman beside him.

The stars came out and a breeze picked up. They'd each eaten their fill. He leaned in and kissed her. "Ready to go in?"

"Ready for you, my love."

He stood and pulled her to her feet.

She kissed his cheek. "I need to bring my bag in from the car."

"I'll clean up while you do that. Do you want to shower?"

She nodded. "See you in a little while."

Collecting everything from the table, he headed for the kitchen. To think he had considered moving just last night. Was he crazy? But then, it had been awesome at the hospital yesterday. That part had made sense. He shrugged and put the left-over pizza in a zip lock bag.

After rinsing the plates and putting them in the dishwasher, he headed into the bedroom to undress. Crawling under the covers, he sat against the headboard, waiting for Lara. Leaning his head back, he sighed loudly. He'd made the right choice. She was the most important thing in his life.

She walked out of the bathroom, her hair wrapped in a towel. "Hey, lover, you up for brushing my hair?"

He reached for the brush she held. "Always."

Hiking up her nightgown, she sat cross-legged between his thighs and took the towel off her hair. "I could get used to this, you know."

He kissed her cheek, loving the way she smelled fresh from the shower. "Fine with me." Choosing a lock of hair, he gently brushed it out. The process relaxed him. It was a tedious job, but something he loved to do.

"*Ahh*." She tilted her head toward him, curving her back and relaxing. "How come it never felt this good when my mom combed out my hair?"

Grinning, he said, "Because she didn't have my sexy legs." He rubbed his foot along her smooth calf.

She clasped his thighs and pulled them closer to her hips. "You're so right."

He drew her hair to the side and trailed kisses across the back of her neck.

She sighed and leaned into him. "I love you, Adam. I don't want to quarrel with you again."

Nipping her shoulder, he grinned. "Me neither." Brushing, he said, "Did you hear about that accident on I-10 yesterday?"

"No, what happened?"

He told her how busy the ER had been—how horribly some people had been hurt. "It reminded me of my time at the Trauma Center in Boston. Crazy hectic, life-threatening injuries, split-second decision making. It was amazing."

"Sounds like you really miss those days." She turned, looking over her shoulder to meet his gaze.

"I admit I do. Working at St. Anne's is a no-brainer, except on very rare occasions. I miss being challenged. A lot."

She drew her brows together. "I didn't realize you were so unhappy."

He shrugged. "I wouldn't say unhappy. Maybe I'm just bored."

Turning around, she said, "My father's practice isn't challenging, either, but I'm not surprised. I always knew what being a small-town attorney would be like. The work is slow-paced, simple stuff—things I can handle in my sleep. There's an upside, though. It's a great job for a woman who also has a family to raise."

He slid his arms around her and whispered in her ear. "Now, I like the sound of that."

She covered his hands with hers. "Me, too. The practice makes a good living for me, and I can still help support my mother until she can draw on her retirement funds. I'm happy where I am."

He finished the last two strands of hair and laid the brush on the nightstand. Turning her around to face him, he said with a grin, "Somebody sassed about make-up sex earlier. I need me some of that."

She moved over and laughed as he took off his shorts.

Lifting her gown, inch by inch, she pulled it over her head. On her knees, naked except for a tiny strip of lace that could hardly be called panties, she curled her finger at him, urging him closer.

Grinning like crazy, he grabbed her butt, pulling her against him.

Running her hands through his hair, she leaned in to kiss him, tasting his lips, twining her tongue with his.

He moaned, clasping her head in his hands, kissing her, then rolling her on her back.

Her beautiful clear-grey eyes looked back at him with such love. He smiled and slid his hips over her.

Her lips lifted in response, and she touched his chest with gentle fingers.

He rotated his pelvis and she grinned. God, how he loved this woman. He took her nipple in his mouth, stroking it with his tongue, sucking more of her breast inside, drawing on it. Cupping her breast in his hand, he loved the fullness of it.

She caressed his cheek, raising her chest, wanting more.

He took her other breast in his mouth, sucking and massaging, as she moaned in pleasure. He hooked his fingers in her panties and drew them down. Drawing them off her feet, he said, "I'm surprised you bother wearing these, they're so tiny."

She grinned. "Don't you like them?"

"Mmm, oh yes, I love them, sweetheart."

She said, "Love this, handsome," and slid down in the bed, between his legs.

Eyes wondering, he rested on his hands as she drew him into her mouth. He groaned as she grasped his hips, sliding him in and out, and sucking hard. He gritted his teeth. Damn, he'd spill inside her if she didn't stop. He sucked in a breath and held still. After a moment he moved in her again, the intense pleasure of the suction, the heat of her mouth, pure ecstasy.

She grabbed his butt, moving him faster and faster.

God, he had to stop. Pulling out of her, he grabbed a condom and quickly rolled it on, then yanked her up and turned her over. She rose to her hands and knees and looked over her shoulder. "I love you, Adam!"

Clasping her hips, nearly out of control, he thrust inside her. She was wet and hot. Hotter than her mouth had been. He bucked again and then again. Sex had never been this good, this perfect, with any other woman.

She pressed against him, bowing her back, giving him access to her core.

He clutched her to him, pounding her, thrusting deep, branding her as his own. His body was rock hard, his blood on fire. Lara was his.

She tensed, cried out, and spasmed around him.

God, she was there. He thrust deep again, his eruption violent, leaving him gasping. He moaned, pulled her up against his chest and kissed her neck, whispering, "I fucking love you, Lara. I love you so much."

She turned her cheek to him. "Adam, I don't have the words for how much I love you."

He kissed her and took her with him down to the bed, spooning her against him. Burying his face in her fragrant hair, he whispered, "I wish this night could last forever."

She drew his fingers to her lips. "It will, in our dreams."

He hugged her closer. He may not be able to make the night last forever, but he could do his best to make their union permanent. Smiling, he snuggled his cheek against her. He had planning to do.

Chapter Thirteen

LARA MET HER MOM THE next day for their standing Wednesday lunch date—one of the ways Lara supported her mother as she dealt with her grief. It got her mom out of the house, and Lara knew the woman loved spending time with her daughter.

After being held up on a conference call, Lara found her mother already seated when she arrived at the little cafe down the street from her office. Pulling out her chair, she said, "I'm sorry I'm late, Mom."

"You don't need to apologize, honey. You're a busy woman. I'm thankful you take time for me like this."

The waitress came and Lara ordered iced tea. Knowing the menu by heart, she left it lying in front of her. "How are you?

Her mom raised her chin. "Missing your daddy, of course, but I'm doing fine."

Lara knew her mother's pride wouldn't let her say anything different, and she still grieved. The devastating blow of losing her husband would take time to get over. Lara clasped her mother's hand. "I'm glad, Momma."

Her mom smiled bravely. "So, tell me what's happening with you. How is that handsome Adam doing?"

Lara knew her mother always had a soft spot for Adam. "He's amazing. We spent the evening at his place last night. Nothing fancy. We ordered a pizza and relaxed."

"Do you think this relationship is serious, honey?"

Lara took a sip of tea. Despite the recent dustup, her feelings for Adam were strong. "I do."

"Oh, sweetheart, I'm so happy."

Unwilling to share details, she changed the subject. "Tell me how your group is going." Her mother had finally joined a grief group and had met some new people who were going through the same thing.

"I think it's helping me." Then she shared some local gossip from the last meeting.

After lunch, Lara headed back to the office. She had another conference call and a stack of documents to go through before the end of the day.

EARLY THE FOLLOWING Saturday afternoon, Lara stepped into her heels and shut her closet door before heading into the kitchen to pour a glass of wine. Adam would be here shortly. They decided to travel to Odessa, seventy-five miles away, for dinner and a movie. When she came back to Ft. Stockton, she couldn't believe there still wasn't a theater in town. Adam had said she could pick the show tonight and she loved Marvel superhero movies so that was what she chose.

The day loomed with angry, rain-filled clouds on the horizon. Storms were forecast for the evening. She stood at her sliding glass doors and sipped her wine. Leaves whisked this way and that across her back yard. A hardy squirrel ran up the nearly-nude tree and peeked over her fence. She definitely needed to call Adam's yardman.

The doorbell rang and she took her glass to the kitchen before grabbing her purse, coat and umbrella. She met him at the door with a kiss. "Do you need an umbrella? I have an extra."

He smiled. "I'll be fine." He wrapped her hand around his arm and escorted her to his truck. After helping her buckle in, he got on the road. "You're beautiful, sweetheart."

"Thank you. You're mighty handsome yourself, cowboy." Though it had been years since he'd lived on the ranch, he still dressed western when they went out. Gorgeous in Wranglers and a hat, one look at the man had her pulse racing. They'd seen each other every evening since she got back from the island. Neither one of them could bear to be apart.

Adam reached for her hand. "How was your day?"

"Lazy. I did absolutely nothing and loved every minute of it. I think I'll hire a housekeeper. I don't have time to do anything anymore."

He nodded. "I have one. She's great. I'll forward her contact to you."

Leaning her head back, she relaxed, visiting with him until they pulled into the parking lot at the theater.

At the entrance, he paid for their tickets and led her inside. "Do you want a snack?"

"I'll take a drink but I don't want to spoil my dinner." She told him what she wanted and waited for him near the entry to the theaters. Women's eyes turned to Adam from all over the room as he walked toward her with her drink. *He's mine, ladies. All mine.*

It had been several years since she'd been to the movies, and she thoroughly enjoyed herself. Adam promised to take her to the next one as the movie ended with an obvious lead to a sequel. Raindrops started to fall as they walked to the truck, and he put his arm around her, urging her into a run.

It was pouring by the time they got to the steakhouse for dinner. Adam raced around the truck and took her umbrella, opening it before he let her step out. They ran inside. Only her legs got wet, but Adam was soaked.

The hostess seated them and he ordered wine. He'd chosen a seat next to her, and leaned in, kissing her from time to time.

She reveled in their closeness. What a loss that she'd lived so many years without him in her life. The leisurely dinner left her satisfied, body and soul.

Out the window, rain still came down. Adam went out first and drove the truck to the entrance, helping her inside and holding her umbrella the whole time. As always, he made her feel cherished.

He climbed in the truck and slammed the door, grinning. "I should have taken that umbrella you offered."

She laughed. "Yeah, tough guy."

Adam pulled out of the parking lot, soon heading out on the state highway leading back to Ft. Stockton.

When he turned on the heater so they could warm up and maybe dry out a little, she leaned back in her seat and relaxed, enjoying her full tummy and being with the man she loved.

Just outside Ft. Stockton Adam glanced at her, then turned back to the road, a crease between his eyes.

She frowned. Why did he look worried? "Is something wrong?"

He didn't answer right away.

"Adam?"

"I got a letter today." He looked at her, his eyes searching hers, then turned back to the road.

"What about?" Something was wrong.

"Before you came back—before I knew anything about you—I applied for several positions at Level I trauma centers in the Dallas area."

Stunned, she sucked in a breath.

Turning to her again, he said. "Right after your father's funeral, I had an interview at one of the hospitals."

"I don't understand. Why didn't you tell me?" Her heart pounded, sending her pulse racing. It was happening again.

His eyes pleaded with her. "I never heard from them. I thought they chose someone else." He looked back at the road. "I didn't keep it from you on purpose. I thought it was irrelevant."

She stared at him. "Is it? Irrelevant?"

He looked at her. "If I go to this interview, and if they hire me, would you marry me and move to Dallas?"

Her jaw dropped. What? He wanted to marry her, but only if she moved to Dallas with him? She shivered, turning to the window. *This is your life, remember? You don't get happy endings.* "Adam, this is all too much. I can't take it in. I'm sorry."

He reached out and touched her shoulder. "I know. This was a huge surprise to me, too. I love you, Lara. Will you at least think about it?"

She nodded, too shattered for tears. When they pulled up at her house, she quickly unbuckled her belt and threw open her door. "Adam, I need to be alone tonight." Grabbing her coat and purse, and leaving her umbrella somewhere on the dark floorboard, she strode to her front door, eighteen and heart-broken all over again.

ADAM WATCHED LARA RUSH into the house, his heart leaden. He wanted to go after her—kiss her until that broken-hearted expression vanished from her face. But he was the last person she would want now. As the door shut behind her, he pulled away from the curb. He'd expected her to be surprised, even happy that he asked her to marry him, but not this upset. Didn't she know how much he loved her?

Of course, he'd love to take the job. But there was still the interview to get through. He'd called and scheduled a time and his flight was booked. The doctor he would be replacing was retiring, and that was why the hospital had taken their time in the past few months filling the position.

When he got home, he fixed himself a drink and headed to bed. Before turning off the light, he texted Lara:

I'm so sorry I upset you. I didn't mean to. I scheduled the interview for Wednesday afternoon. I don't know if they'll even offer me the job. Lara, I love you. Please, be patient with me.

A few minutes later, she responded:

Adam, I love you. I know you and understand you need to do this. Good luck.

He sighed. She wished him good luck. That was something. If only she would go with him. She'd lived in the city for years in California and been happy. Surely, she'd enjoy living in Dallas. No more driving seventy-five miles to see a movie, or four hours to catch a flight. Leaving her father's business and her mother would be a big deal for Lara, though. Would she be willing to do that? It was asking a hell of a lot from her.

He swallowed some whiskey. It was inconceivable that he would live without her. Before her, his life had been so cold—emotionless. He didn't want to go on without the warmth, the pleasure, the love she brought into his life.

But, the excitement and challenge of a trauma center like the one in Dallas was something he'd missed terribly. The unfortunate accident on the freeway showed him just how much. St. Anne's ER couldn't offer anything remotely similar.

He finished the rest of his whiskey and turned out the lamp. There had to be an answer.

LARA LAY IN BED, HER thoughts whirling. How had she let this happen to her again? Of course, Adam would choose the trauma center job. He'd sworn he loved her when he was eighteen, and yet he'd moved to Boston. She was stupid to think he had changed. He professed his love now but wanted this job in Dallas, knowing her place was here in Ft. Stockton, running her father's practice and supporting her mother as she dealt with her grief. It was unbelievable that she'd fallen for the same damn scenario.

Turning on her side, she clutched a pillow to her belly. The man couldn't be depended on. That much was obvious. He'd abandoned her in the past. Why hadn't she stayed away from him? How stupid could she be?

And what the hell kind of marriage proposal was that? Marry me and move to Dallas? It was ridiculous that the first time those words came from his mouth a huge transition was thrown in with them. That's not how it was supposed to work. You proposed because you loved someone, not because you wanted them to follow you somewhere.

Dammit. She bit her lip, the enormity of her loss hitting her. She'd trusted him. Again. This betrayal was so much worse because of that. Her heart, full of love that she couldn't help, felt torn in two. She pressed her face into the pillow as tears filled her eyes. She hadn't seen this coming. But she should have. It was Adam, after all.

Chapter Fourteen

LARA HURRIED TO THE diner to meet her mother for their Wednesday lunch date. After another night of little sleep, Lara felt scatter-brained and tired. Her mother was seated when Lara walked in and she strode over and took a seat. "Sorry I'm late, Mom. I say that every time, now." She dropped her purse on the floor and put her head in her hands, ready to throw in the towel on the day, and it was only half over.

"Oh, honey, don't worry about that. Really. I enjoy our lunches so much. I appreciate you making time for me when you're always so busy." Her mother clasped Lara's arm until she looked up. "You look tired, sweetheart. Aren't you getting any sleep? I swear, those bags under your eyes are awful."

Lara sighed and sat back in her chair. "They do look terrible, don't they? My concealer isn't touching them."

Her mother leaned forward, her eyes dark with worry. "What is it honey? What's going on?"

Lara blew out a breath. "It's Adam. I don't know what to do. I feel like ..."

"What, sweetheart?"

In a shaking voice, Lara told her about the job application, the interview, how Adam wanted her to marry him and move, that he would leave her again just like before if she didn't go.

Her mother moved to sit beside her. "Honey, I know you love Adam—really love him, right?"

Lara dabbed at her eyes with a napkin and nodded.

"Sweetheart, you go with him. You don't need to stay here for me. I've got my group, and I'm so much better now. As far as running your father's business, we can work that out. We'll find someone to buy it. That shouldn't be too hard. There are plenty of young lawyers who would love to get their hands on an existing client base. Sure, your daddy always wanted you to have his legacy but, more than anything, he wanted his baby girl to be happy. And this Adam, he makes you happy."

She hugged Lara and continued. "You call your man. Tell him you'll marry him and follow him to the ends of this earth if that's where he wants to go. You hear me, honey?"

Lara leaned her head on her mother's shoulder, feeling like a little girl again. Her momma had just made everything all better. "Thank you, Mom. I love you."

ADAM BOARDED HIS FLIGHT home from Dallas. The interview had gone well, and the job was his. He'd asked for a few days to think over their proposal. It was a great offer though the pay didn't equal what he made when he worked in Boston. However, the cost of living was much higher back east, too. Now, he had to get serious—decide whether he'd take the hospital up on their job.

Lara had asked for a break. Other than their texts that same evening he hadn't talked with her since their date Saturday night. He missed her terribly. After his announcement, it was only fair to give her time to think but it had been so hard to go on day after day without her. He had to see her, but first he had to sort this whole job thing out.

AFTER ARRIVING HOME in the middle of the night, Adam slept in late Thursday morning. He got up, fixed a cup of coffee and stood at the sliding doors. It was cold and windy outside. The pool guy had treated and covered the pool for the winter. The yard appeared tired and sad without it. Adam was off today and tomorrow. Hopefully he wouldn't be called in.

He sat on the couch, taking a swallow of coffee and noticed that Lara had left behind one of her colorful scarves. On windy days she tied one over her hair to keep it from tangling so badly. Holding it to his nose, he inhaled the sweet scent of her shampoo and a bit of her citrusy cologne. All at once, his need for her overwhelmed him, proving that a life without her was impossible. He couldn't go to Dallas if she wouldn't move with him. Somehow, he'd known that, but now it was viscerally real.

He sniffed again, letting her scent fill his head. It was wrong to take Lara away from her mother. The woman needed her daughter to make it through this time of loss. And asking Lara to give up her father's law practice, her inheritance, was an awful thing to do. He should never have considered it. She would be turning her back on everything and everyone who mattered to her if she followed him to Dallas. He'd been a selfish bastard to ask that of her.

He loved her—wanted to marry her—and Ft. Stockton was a perfect place to raise their children. So what if the ER at St. Anne's wasn't the most interesting job in the world. Maybe, later in their marriage, he could take a Level I trauma position.

If not, he'd still have the woman he loved and his whole family surrounding him.

He wrapped the scarf around his hand and smiled. It was time to talk to Lara.

AFTER A QUICK SHOWER, he headed straight to the florist's where he ordered a huge vase of Lara's favorite roses and had them delivered to her office. His next stop was at the jewelry store his family had used for ages. They always had a good selection of settings and stones. He browsed for a while before finding exactly the setting he wanted, then had the sales person bring out a selection of diamonds. After choosing the perfect stone, he asked how long before the ring could be ready, explaining his urgency. The woman smiled and, after gathering her merchandise, headed back to ask the jeweler.

A few minutes later he came up to the counter and shook Adam's hand. "I understand there's a rush on this purchase?"

Adam smiled. "There is. I don't know the size, but I'd like to give it to her tonight, if she'll have me."

The jeweler grinned. "Give me until five, Adam. It's not often a Govain son asks for wedding rings."

Adam thrust out his hand. "Thanks. I owe you one. I'll be back before you close."

Back in his truck, he sent Lara a text:

I'm desperate to see you tonight. I'm off today and can make dinner by seven. What do you say, my love?

She must be busy, because she didn't respond. He'd looked up the recipe at home and had his grocery list. So, he stopped by the store and picked up everything he needed for dinner. He was making a delicious French onion soup made with white wine, both chicken and beef broths, and lots of gruyere cheese. He also bought a fruit platter and would serve the soup with toasted French bread. With the cold, drizzly afternoon, this would be the perfect meal.

She finally answered:

I'll be there. Thank you.

When he got home, he put the groceries away and sat down with a drink. He had to speak his heart perfectly tonight. Lara was hurt and rightfully so. He must overcome that and prove to her that she was more important than anything else in his life. She felt he hadn't considered her love a priority when he left for college in Boston. He couldn't let that happen again. There could be no doubt in her mind that he loved her completely—that she was his everything. That he couldn't live without her. Tonight, he had to find the right words to convince her of his love.

His thoughts moved from one point to the next as he slowly drank his whiskey. By the time he should start dinner, he was ready.

LARA RANG THE DOORBELL as he dumped the toasted bread into a basket. He covered it with a towel to keep the bread warm and strode to the door to let her in. She was sexy yet professional in her skirted black suit.

As she came inside, she put her arms around his neck and kissed him. "I missed you, Adam. I'm so glad you called." She smiled and stepped past him.

This greeting was much sweeter than he anticipated. "I missed you too, honey. Head to the kitchen and I'll pour you some wine." As he filled her glass with pinot noir, he examined her and, dammit, she looked terrible. He was a fucking asshole, putting her through hell this past week. He handed her a glass and cupped her face. "Sweetheart, I want to say so much, but let's eat first, okay?"

She nodded, a tiny smile lighting up her eyes. "I need to talk to you, too, Adam."

Was that a good thing or a bad thing? Now he was worried. "Why don't you sit at the table, and I'll bring out the food." He made several trips, then sat down next to her. "I can't wait to taste this soup. My stomach growled the whole time I was cooking it."

She smiled. "It smells fabulous."

He kept up light conversation during dinner, scrupulously avoiding the elephant in the room. When they'd finished, he picked up the dishes. "I'm off tomorrow, so I'll clean up in the morning. Why don't you head to the living room, and I'll bring the wine?"

Hands shaking slightly now that the time had come, he dumped the dishes in the sink. So much rested on the next few minutes. He closed his eyes and prayed—something he should do more often. Tossing the hand towel on the cabinet, he strode toward his fate.

Lara sat on the couch, her back straight.

He refilled her glass and did the same for his. Sitting next to her, he reached for her hand. "Lara, I know what I want to say to you, I just pray I get it right."

She clutched his hand. "Please, Adam, can I talk first?" Her lips trembled, and she licked them.

Oh, God. What did this mean? "Of course, honey. Whatever you need." Heart pounding, he stared into her eyes, hoping for a hint as to what she would say.

She swallowed, her throat spasming visibly. "Adam, I love you more than anything or anyone. Nothing is more important to me than you. My mother assures me that she will be just fine without me. She's agreed that we'll sell my father's practice. She sends her best wishes and her love." Lara looked into his eyes. "Adam, I'll marry you and move to Dallas."

He sucked in a breath, unable to believe that she would give up everything to be with him—leave her grieving mother and sell what her father had worked his whole life to build. It was an incredible honor and a terrible tragedy. He pulled her into his arms. "Oh, honey, I love you. I don't want you to leave your momma or sell your father's business. I'm not taking the job. I want to live here in Ft. Stockton and marry you. I want to raise our children here, around our family where they can play with their cousins and get spoiled by their grandparents. Maybe someday, when our children are grown, I'll take a job somewhere else. But not now."

Lara burst into tears, and he held her tight, smothering her with kisses. He'd finally made the right choice.

Chapter Fifteen

LARA MARVELED AT THE gorgeous white-lace wedding dress hanging from her bathroom door. The beautiful gown had a stylish tulle illusion scooped neck featuring an off-the-shoulder lace border with a plunging illusion back teamed with an A-line skirt and full-length lace sleeves. It hugged her waist and hips, flowing to the floor in a curling train. A matching floor-length veil would cover her long, dark hair.

The limo would be here in less than thirty minutes to pick her up. Her makeup and hair were already done.

Eve, her Matron of Honor, walked into the bedroom. "Ready to put on your dress, honey?" She smiled, looking gorgeous in her yellow-gold gown.

"Yes, it's time." The wedding flowers, Lara's favorite yellow roses with orange tips, would look beautiful with Eve's dress—one of the reason's Lara had picked it out when they'd gone dress shopping in Dallas.

Lara's mother was at the church making sure that everything was perfect for the ceremony. She'd stopped by early this morning and had coffee with Lara before heading over.

Eve took down the dress and began unbuttoning the long line of buttons running down the sheer back, careful not to snag the delicate material.

Lara shifted from foot to foot—five months of hectic planning had all come down to the next few hours. Caleb was best man. Lara's mother had asked her good friend if the woman's young grandson and granddaughter could be the ring bearer and flower girl. Their mother had agreed. Lara's colors were yellow-gold and spring green—perfect for her April twentieth wedding date. The reception would be held at the country club where her parents had been members forever.

Eve finished with the buttons and carefully helped slip the dress over Lara's head.

She slid her arms into the long off-the-shoulder sleeves, feeling sexy and elegant at the same time.

Eve smoothed the material over Lara's curves then began the tedious process of buttoning the back of the dress. "Dylan got here a few minutes ago. He had a flat tire on the way from El Paso and freaked out, thinking he might miss his big brother's wedding."

Eve frowned. "That's awful. I'm glad he got here in time. I wish he could have come sooner so we could spend some time together, but I understand he can't miss his college classes."

When Eve was done, Lara slipped on her white satin heels and looked at herself in the mirror. Smiling, she imagined what Adam would feel when he saw her.

Eve picked up the back of her dress as Lara grabbed her small white bag. Eve said, "Ready, you beautiful bride?"

Lara grinned. "Let's go." The limo waited out front and, as Caleb had come earlier to pick up her luggage, all she had to do was walk out the door.

ADAM, IN HIS BLACK tux, stood on the raised dais, Caleb at his side. He shifted from foot to foot and glanced down the aisle for the fiftieth time. The organ played quietly in the background, and a buzz of low conversation came from the crowd of friends and family gathered in the pews. The church was full of Lara's favorite yellow and orange flowers and bright green ribbons. The rich aroma from the huge bouquet sitting on the table behind him reminded him of her. His father, Roy, was giving Lara away, making this wedding day even more special.

The pastor stopped at the organist and whispered something to her, then ascended the steps to the pulpit and stood behind the lectern. Suddenly, the chords to *The Wedding March* rang out.

Adam's heart leapt, then began to pound. His gaze swept to the entrance to the church, eagerly anticipating the arrival of his beautiful Lara.

First came the precious little five-year-old flower girl in her white lace dress, followed just a step behind by the slightly bewildered-looking four-year-old ring bearer. Eve came next, walking with slow, smooth steps.

At last, an absolutely stunning Lara turned down the aisle on his father's arm. His jaw dropped. Her gorgeous dress hugged her curves, her small waist begging him to encase it with his hands. No woman had ever looked more perfect at her wedding.

Lara met his wondering gaze and smiled.

Grinning, he clasped his hands behind him. Damn, he was the luckiest man in the world. Each step she took, brought certainty to him. He would never regret his choice to remain in Ft. Stockton.

Lara climbed the steps to him.

The reverend asked, "Who gives this woman's hand in marriage?"

His father answered, "I do," and placed Lara's hand in Adam's.

As his father retreated down the steps, the reverend moved to the center of the dais and said, "Mr. Govain, Miss Cole, stand before me please."

Adam tucked Lara's hand under his arm and led her to stand directly in front of the reverend, who now stood free of the lectern.

The preacher began, "We have come together to celebrate the union in Christian love of Lara and Adam. Today they will unite their hearts and their lives. This is possible because of the love God has created in them, through Jesus Christ."

Lara turned to Adam and smiled.

He squeezed her hand, overwhelmed with his love for her. Everything had led them to this day.

The reverend held their gazes and continued. "Two lives are not united by ceremony, but only in the power, love, and grace of God. As God demonstrated His love in Jesus, our Lord, Adam and Lara will demonstrate this God-given love by giving themselves to one another."

He nodded to each of them. "Adam and Lara, no other human ties are more tender, no other vows are more sacred than these you are about to assume. You are entering into that holy estate which is the deepest mystery of experience, and which is the very sacrament of divine love."

Lara leaned against him, as if needing his touch.

He squeezed her fingers gently.

Holding Adam's gaze, the reverend said, "Adam, will you have Lara to be your wedded wife, from this day forward, in sickness and in health, until you part in death?"

Adam spoke up strongly, "I will," and looked at Lara.

She smiled up at him.

The reverend turned to Lara. "Lara, will you have Adam to be your wedded husband from this day forward, in sickness and in health, until you part in death?"

She said, "I will."

"Adam, please take Lara by her right hand, and say your vows to your bride."

Adam clasped her hand and smiled, looking deep into her beautiful grey eyes. "Lara, I promise always to be true. I will grow with you and build with you a better life as we learn to be patient, kind, giving and to cherish each day together. As your husband, I am yours, and today I deliver to you my heart, forever."

Lara, tears brimming in her eyes, squeezed his hand and smiled.

The reverend turned to Lara. "Please repeat your vows to Adam."

Lara said, "Adam, I love you without fear, without hesitation, and promise to support you, encourage, and cherish you as your wife. I will always be on your side. Always. Live with me, laugh with me, love with me, and I'll be your devoted wife forever."

He shivered as the depth of her pledge sunk in. She would devote herself to him, but he must cherish her even more. He promised himself now, before God, to be up to that challenge.

The reverend turned to Adam. "Adam, what symbol do you bring as a pledge of the sincerity of your vows?"

He replied, "A ring."

The reverend met Lara's gaze. "Please remember, a ring is more than a symbol of your marriage, Lara. It's a seal of the vow you have made to one another. The circle of the ring is, as far as human eyes can see, a perfect circle—with no beginning or end—so God, too, has perfect love for you and wants you to love one another in His grace—never, never ending. This ring is made of precious metal. You are also precious in God's sight and now in the life of Adam. When you are absent from one another, the presence of the ring reminds you to be faithful and to fulfill your vows to Adam."

Adam slipped his ring on Lara's finger, looking into her eyes, a sense of overwhelming love flooding through him. He clasped her hand tightly.

The reverend smiled. "Lara, what symbol do you bring as a pledge of the sincerity of your vows?"

Lara said, "A ring."

He turned to Adam. "Adam, this ring is a seal of Lara's vow to you. She presents this to you as a token of her love for you in Jesus Christ. Your role is one of leadership and privilege as head of your family. You must lead in worship, works, and fellowship. Lara depends upon you for strength."

Adam swallowed. He would be strong for her. He would never, ever let her down and he would lead her, and their family, with his strength and love for the rest of his life.

Lara slid Adam's ring on his finger.

He had never felt closer to her. Staring into her eyes, eternity didn't seem long enough to love her.

The reverend smiled and looked at them both. "For as much as Adam and Lara have consented in holy wedlock, confirming this by giving and receiving a ring, by the authority given unto me as a minister of the Church of Jesus Christ, I now declare you husband and wife, according to God and the laws of the state of Texas. Adam, you may kiss your bride."

Adam slipped his arms around her and pulled her close, claiming her lips in a scorching kiss, branding her with his love that would last until his death.

She kissed him back, wrapping her arms around his neck, giving herself wholly to him.

When at last he ended the kiss, she looked at him with tears in her eyes. He whispered, "I love you, darling," and turned to face their friends and family, holding their clasped hands in the air.

Applause broke out around them as they stepped down from the dias. Grinning, Adam acknowledged people on both sides of the aisle as he led Lara by the hand toward the door. If only there wasn't the reception at the country club. He was ready to start his honeymoon!

Chapter Sixteen

LARA TURNED ON HER back, already having absorbed enough sun on her front as she lay on a comfortable lounge chair on the secluded beach. This was the first day of their seven-day Caribbean honeymoon on Punta Cana Island, and it was proving to be as fantastic as she had imagined. She and Adam had booked a two-bedroom house right on the beach at the exclusive Resort. There were six restaurants with world-class chefs in the complex so they could eat in or go out on the town and have wonderful food either way.

Tomorrow, Adam had them scheduled at the spa and wellness center for a day of pampering to set the tone for the rest of their stay. While on the island, they would also go snorkeling on the reef, paddle board, spend part of a day at the ecological park, and take a romantic sunset cruise. Most of all, though, they would relax and recover from the stress leading up to the wedding.

A shadow covered her face and she opened her eyes. A resort employee held the piña colada she'd ordered. "Gracìas." Adam was working out in the gym and would join her later on the beach. They'd arrived very early in the morning and had collapsed into bed, saving their romantic honeymoon night for this evening. Dinner would be at the elegant Bamboo Restaurant where they served Mediterranean-influenced food from their own organic gardens.

She sipped her drink, eyes still closed, and enjoyed the breeze blowing in off the ocean. The sound of the waves breaking lulled her. The resort had miles of private beach and few people were at the water.

Someone plopped into the chair beside her, and she turned her head.

Adam grinned. "Hello, sweetheart. Miss me?"

"Always," and she leaned over for a kiss.

He smacked her lips and pulled her closer, smothering her in a hard, melting kiss, leaving her breathless.

She smiled and drew back.

Grabbing her hand and pulling her up as he stood, he headed for the water. "Let's get wet."

She trotted beside him as he strode out into the waves.

Wrapping his arm around her waist, he drew her in for another kiss. "I love you, Lara." The water was up to her chest and Adam steadied her.

"I love you more." She looked into his eyes and found adoration staring back at her. She pulled his head down and kissed him thoroughly, nipping his lip before letting him go. "Tonight, I'll show you just how much."

He threw his head back and hooted, grinning. "Now that's what I'm talking about."

Fish nibbled at her calves, tickling her. "Do you feel that?"

"The fish? Yep."

She grinned. "Let's hope they're the only things down there."

He laughed. "I have plans tonight for the parts of you under this water. Any sharks are fish bait."

Pulling his head down to her, she kissed him, twining her tongue with his, showing him how much she desired him.

He lifted her and she wrapped her legs around his waist as he walked into deeper water. The waves now broke at his chest. The powerful water pushed at him, and yet he held her firmly in place. Waves washed over her back as he kissed her, exploring her mouth, teasing her lips, letting his love for her pour out of him.

She relaxed—immersing herself in the sensation of the water washing back and forth across her body and in the love flowing into her from the man of her dreams. Adam's hands caressed her as his mouth made her his.

When at last he walked her back to shore, she was completely in tune with him as he eased her down in her chair.

He laid down beside her and closed his eyes. "I love you. You'll never know how much."

She reached for his hand. "I do know, and I love you the same, sweetheart." Closing her eyes, she relaxed knowing that her beloved would sleep next to her. She was safe.

ADAM LOOKED UP FROM his dinner, his eyes caressing the curves of Lara's face. Just a little while longer, and he'd have her in bed. Her formfitting strapless dress had held his attention captive from the moment she put it on.

She smiled, grey eyes flashing, knowing just what he was thinking.

He grinned and took her hand. "You're gorgeous. Eat fast. I want you in my bed!"

She laughed and squeezed his fingers.

He sat next to her, rather than across from her, needing the closeness. Running his hand up the soft skin of her arm, he kissed her shoulder. Let people talk. This was his honeymoon. He could make a scene if he wanted to. Goosebumps appeared on Lara's shoulder and he grinned. Whispering in her ear, he said, "You'll have goosebumps all over you before I get through with you tonight."

She bit her lip, covering a smile. "Same to you, buddy."

He laughed and took a swallow of wine. The food was wonderful, but it hardly whetted his appetite. What he wanted sat beside him, not on his plate. He imagined the taste of her on his tongue, and his mouth watered. God, how he loved her.

She sipped her wine, watching him. "A penny for your thoughts?"

He grinned wickedly. "Too naughty for public consumption."

She laughed. "You're terrible, Adam Govain."

Downing another swallow of wine, his eyes traveled over the swell of her breasts in the royal-blue dress's low-cut neckline. He imagined his hands on them and his cock jerked. Shoving another bite of food in his mouth, he looked to see how much was left on Lara's plate. They were both about halfway through dinner. He groaned silently and swallowed. After his next bite, he said, "You're not eating much. Aren't you hungry?"

"I'm just taking my time. The food is delicious." She took a forkful.

He ate another bite. *Calm down, 'bro. Let her eat.*

An interminable thirty minutes later, he paid the bill and helped Lara from her chair. She had turned down dessert, thank God. His senses heightened as he walked her toward their house. Her lovely perfume excited him, making his cock hard. He settled his arm around her shoulders and her soft skin under his fingertips sent sensual waves of pleasure through him. Her hip brushed him and his belly tightened, sending an erotic message to harden his chest and nipples. By the time they walked through the front door, he was way past ready to fuck her.

As soon as the door shut behind them, he turned and shoved Lara against it, kissing her deeply, running his hands over her body, then pulling her away enough to draw down her zipper. The pretty blue dress fell to the floor, leaving her in only a tiny pair of panties. He knelt and sucked on first one taut nipple and then the other.

She moaned, head thrown back, legs spread, as his hands roved over her secret places.

He loved that she threw herself into lovemaking—held nothing from him. Standing, he yanked at his tie, removing it, along with his shirt. His chest expanded with a deep breath as he dominated the space between them.

Lara unbuckled his belt and unfastened his slacks, sliding both his briefs and slacks down his hips.

Grinning, he kicked off his shoes and stepped out of his pants. His cock proudly pointed to the heavens. He would make her scream his name.

Lara went to her knees and took him in her mouth, sucking hard, stroking up and down.

She was exquisite—he almost came in an instant. Taking a breath, he made the sensation fade. Clasping her face, he closed his eyes, letting her have her way with him.

Her tongue worked him and her lips created a suction that nearly drove him wild. He rode waves of pleasure that grew stronger and stronger. His world centered on her mouth and his cock.

Suddenly, it was too much. He pulled back before he blew inside her. Drawing her to her feet, he kissed her, eating at her mouth, stroking her with the velvet lash of his tongue, nibbling with lips and teeth. Savoring her. "Come on, baby. Let's go." He picked her up and carried her to the bedroom, pulling the covers back before laying her on the bed. Taking hold of her panties, he quickly slid them off, his lips parting as he pulled air into his lungs in a near pant. He could sense the need radiating off her.

She smiled trustingly at him. "I love you, Adam. I always will."

"Honey, you're everything to me." He slid her thighs apart and climbed between them, laying her legs over his shoulders. Spreading her, using the tip of his tongue, he circled her sensitive clit then licked it.

She gasped and stiffened.

He did it again and she moaned. Slipping two fingers inside her, he licked her again, and gently sucked.

She arched her hips.

He continued to play with her, eliciting cries and moans until Lara begged him, "Please, now, Adam."

He sucked one last time and, with her legs over his shoulders, rose and thrust inside her.

She clutched the sheets. "Adam!" Panting, she cried out with each deep thrust as her pleasure climbed. She reached for him. "Now!"

She was hot and Christ she was gorgeous. He loved it when she lost control. He pulled out of her and lifted her off the bed and set her on her feet beside it. Bending her over, he drew her to him and thrust inside her. Rolling his hips, he stroked deep, caressing her with his length. His lips touched her ear and he whispered, "Give it to me, babe."

She moaned. "Oh, God. I love you." She cocked her hips, bowed her back, gave him access to her core.

Pumping hard, he rasped, "I love you, sweetheart." She felt so good—so perfect. Every muscle in his body was tied to her—a part of her. His skin was so hot he burned. He was close, so close. He couldn't hold off much longer.

Lara gasped. "Adam!" She spasmed in ripples around him and her knees went weak.

He exploded inside her, shudders racking his body, and he grunted from the pure animal satisfaction of his release. Lara moaned and he held her to him. Languid now, he pulled her with him and climbed in bed, cuddling her to his chest. As she turned her head and sighed, he kissed her temple. Lara was the piece that had been missing in his life. Holding her tight, he kissed her again. "I love you, honey, and I always will."

She smiled, clasping the arm that surrounded her. "Forever, sweetheart," and she brought his fingertips to her lips.

He closed his eyes. His life was complete.

Epilogue

LARA FINISHED WRAPPING the last birthday present. Her baby turned one today. She couldn't believe how fast the year had gone. At first there were sleepless nights. It had taken a while for her milk to come in, but after that, things had gotten better, thank God. Managing her father's busy practice as a new mother had been no easy feat. She'd pumped her breasts twice a day. That took care of two feedings on Adam's part. Her sitter had brought the baby into the office to nurse around one-thirty each day. Lara had loved getting to see her little one while she worked.

Adam was an absolutely perfect father. He hadn't minded taking his share of the night-time feedings, and he became an expert diaper changer. And now that their little one ate baby food, he excelled at making an airplane fly into a little mouth.

Adam walked in the living room and wrapped her in his arms from behind, nibbling on her neck until it tickled. "Looks like you're done."

She grinned. "I am. All's ready for the party. Thanks for all your help, honey."

Turning her to face him, he kissed her tenderly. "Of course. This is a big day." Mewling sounds came from the baby monitor. "Somebody's waking up. I'll go."

Lara smiled and stepped away. This daddy sure loved his baby. He was such a help, and Lara seldom needed to ask.

He came back into the room, bouncing their little girl in his arms, her soft dark curls a stark contrast to Adams white shirt. He kissed her and she laughed, turning clear grey eyes to him. "Who's daddy's pretty girl?" Bouncing her again, he grinned. "It's my sweet Grace. That's right."

Lara headed toward them, her happiness overflowing as it always did when she saw them together—her two most precious people on earth. Having Grace didn't erase the loss of Lara's first daughter. Nothing would do that. But having this new child with Adam was a joy like no feeling she'd ever experienced. She hugged him and kissed Grace's little cheek. Though Lara's journey had been dark and long, this perfect ending, God's wonderful blessing, eclipsed those black days. Her future was built on joy in her little family and endless love.

ACKNOWLEDGEMENTS

1. SUANNE SCHAFER, D.O.– Many thanks to Suanne for her advice on all things medical. Dr. Adam couldn't have existed without her. Any mistakes in medicinal details are entirely my own.

BONUS CHAPTER
THE COWBOY'S WISH,
BOOK 3

DYLAN GOVAIN DALLIED his rope to the saddle horn and slid his tall bay gelding to a stop in a cloud of dust. The calf hit the end of the slack and spun toward him. Pivoting his horse, he dragged the calf toward the cowboys who would brand and inoculate him. The cows and bull would go through the portable head gate for their shots and deworming, but the youngest calves were too small for the big metal contraption.

The heat of the June sun penetrated the denim of his long-sleeved shirt and sweat pooled on his chest and back. He took a minute to remove his hat and wipe moisture from his brow while the ranch hands went to work. The calf bawled loudly as the branding iron sizzled against his hide. A second cowboy gave him a shot. Before he was set free, the little bull calf received a quick spray of dewormer between his shoulders.

Dylan rode back into the herd, his eye already on another calf. After four years of college and more classes to achieve his teaching certificate, he was finally home. He'd missed being horseback and the day-to-day chores of working cattle. However, he didn't plan on spending the rest of his life taking orders from his big brother, Caleb, who ran the 263,000-acre ranch now that his dad was semi-retired. That was why Dylan had trained to teach Agricultural Education, or Ag, to high school kids.

Teachers sure didn't get rich, but he felt a calling. If young people didn't learn the skills they needed to be successful at farming and ranching, the way of life Dylan loved would fade away. He wanted to do his part to motivate the next generation to choose living on the land as their future.

By the end of the afternoon, the herd had been inoculated and dewormed, and the fence panels loaded and sent on their way back to the barn. Dylan hung back from the line of vehicles, letting the dust settle from the truck and trailer in front of him. A day like today left him tired out but satisfied. Sleep would come easily tonight.

Tomorrow he wouldn't be working on the ranch. His dad had his annual cardiology check-up, and Dylan was driving him. Roy said he could drive himself, but that wasn't happening. What if he got bad news? After suffering a life-threatening heart attack years ago, nobody took Roy's health for granted.

When Dylan got back to the ranch, he unsaddled the gelding and washed him off with the hose. The horse jiggled the skin on his back and sides, enjoying his bath. After settling him in his stall for the night, Dylan headed into the house, ready for a cool shower before dinner.

As he opened the front door, baby talk came from near the stairs, and soon his little niece Abi came toddling around the corner.

Her face lit up, and she raised her arms, running toward him. "Dilwan, Dilwan."

He laughed and knelt to pick her up. "How's my pretty girl?" Planting a kiss on her soft cheek, he continued into the family room.

His sister-in-law, Eve, stood, her phone to her ear. "Okay. I'll see you in a few minutes." She hung up. "Well, someone found her favorite cowboy."

Dylan laughed. "She sure did. Met me at the door."

"When she saw I was on the phone, she scooted out of here. I figured she couldn't get in much trouble while I talked to Caleb for a second."

He knelt and put his niece down. "I stink. I need a shower."

Abi clung to him and cried.

Laughing, he peeled her little fingers from his shirt and gave her a kiss. "I'll be back in a jiffy, sweetheart."

Eve picked up her daughter and hugged her, and the tot quieted.

Abi got her fair hair from her father and had huge blue eyes. It was obvious that the little girl would grow up just as gorgeous as her tawny-haired mother though Eve had striking golden eyes. Caleb would have his hands full when his daughter took an interest in boys.

Dylan eventually joined the family at the dinner table and found that his mother, Millie, along with his dad, had been invited. Dylan gave his mom a peck on the cheek. "Hey, how was your day?"

"Fabulous. I didn't do a thing but read my romance novel, and I don't feel a bit guilty. A woman has to take a day off once in a while."

He grinned. "I'm glad you're taking care of yourself, Mom. You should take a day to relax more often. You're retired, too, you know."

Though his dad still went out on the ranch every day, he was never horseback, and he left the overall management to Caleb. This setup had been a hard transition for Roy after his heart attack, but a necessary one.

"So, Dad, I'll pick you up at ten tomorrow."

"I don't see why I need to keep going back to the damn cardiologist when I'm feeling just fine," Roy grumped.

"Don't even think about backing out of this appointment, Roy Govain," Millie said firmly. "You promised you'd take care of yourself, and I'm holding you to it."

"I'm going, I'm going." Roy gave a long-suffering sigh and shoved a bite of steak in his mouth.

Millie smiled and rubbed his shoulder, the affection between them obvious.

Dylan hoped his eventual marriage would be as happy as the one his parents shared. His father had been a wild cowboy far longer than most young men, but Millie had tamed him. Theirs was a relationship based on love and mutual respect.

After dinner, when he said goodbye to his parents, Dylan couldn't help but notice how they'd aged. His father had stayed a bachelor until he was thirty-four, and his mother was seven years younger. Though Caleb and Adam came early on in their marriage, Dylan was way younger than his nearest brother, Adam. Somehow, Dylan couldn't get used to the idea that his parents had gotten old. He gave his mother an especially-gentle kiss goodbye and hugged his father before closing the door behind them.

LENNIE DUNCAN EYED the fast-approaching door to the cardiologist's office. It was a royal pain to maneuver through.

Before she could decide whether to back in or ask her father grab the door, Dylan Govain opened it and stepped outside. "Let me get this for you." He smiled as he held it wide enough to allow her father's chair to enter.

She pressed her lips together and nodded her thanks, her heart pounding at the sight of the good-looking cowboy. Dammit, why did she always react to him this way? The Govains were persona non grata to the Duncans due to a land dispute between their great great-grandfathers which still caused problems for the Duncans today. The old saying that time heals all wounds definitely did not apply in this instance.

Roy Govain gave her father a curt nod and looked back down at his magazine as she rolled her dad up to the receptionist's window to check him in.

Her father huffed and turned away. There was no love lost between the two men.

After signing her father's name, she wheeled him to the opposite side of the room and sat beside his chair.

Refusing a magazine, her father stared out the window, obviously irritated to share the room with the Govains.

Lennie glanced at Dylan out of the corner of her eye. They were the same age so he must be through with college, too. Crap, he was hot. Though not as tall as his older brothers, his six-foot frame was all handsome cowboy. Soft brown eyes tried to catch her attention, though she kept lowering hers beneath her lashes. Word was he could have gone pro with his saddle-bronc riding, but chose to pursue teaching instead. Wait until the gossip mill found out he was back. Tongues would wag and women would primp in front of mirrors.

A nurse opened the back-office door and called Roy's name. Dylan glanced her way, then stood. Before following his father through the door, he looked over his shoulder. "Nice seeing you, Lennie." Grinning, he closed the door behind him.

Damned if her heart didn't pick up its beat. She clenched her teeth and grabbed a magazine. Why did it have to be this guy, the one person who was off limits, that made her pulse race? No man had done that for her since she broke up with Nic at A&M. Dylan had always gone out of his way to speak to her in school though she hadn't given him the time of day. What was the point? Her father would never have allowed her to date a Govain.

She flipped through the pages of the magazine without really seeing them. Dylan had been an outgoing, confident guy in school and outrageously good at bronc riding. He went to the high school national finals every year and had taken the buckle and saddle his senior year.

He'd had his choice of girls back then, which made it all the more surprising that he tried to connect with her so often. He even asked her to their junior prom, though he said it jokingly, and she didn't think he was serious. How could he have been serious when he knew the way their fathers felt about each other? However, she'd always wondered, had he been sincere in his invitation?

The back-office door opened and the nurse called her father's name. As the woman led them down the hallway, the doctor entered a room on the right.

Dylan caught her eye from inside and nodded, a smile creasing his handsome face.

She returned the smile without thinking then mentally kicked herself. That cowboy didn't need to be encouraged. Following the nurse into a room, Lennie put Dylan Govain out of her mind. Her father, his stroke, and whether he would get better were all that mattered now.

DYLAN DROVE HOME FROM the cardiologist's office, his thoughts racing. Seeing Lennie there was the last thing he'd expected. Once they had some privacy back in the treatment room, he asked his father why Lennie's dad was in a wheelchair. His father explained that Evan Duncan had suffered a serious stroke several months before. Dylan had noticed that part of Evan's face sagged, and his hand curled in on itself. His prematurely-aged face was heartbreaking. Evan couldn't be more than fifty. Roy had said that, as far as he knew, Lennie was running things at the ranch now.

Dylan reached over and patted his dad's shoulder. "Glad you checked out okay today. I want you around for a long time to come."

Roy nodded. "I plan on it, Son."

Poor Lennie. She must be heartsick over her father's illness. How was she holding up with handling everything at the ranch on her own? She would have just graduated, too. She'd attended A&M while he'd gone to Stephenville to Tarleton State.

Lennie was as gorgeous as ever. She still let her shoulder-length blonde hair hang naturally and bangs framed her blue eyes. Instead of downplaying her mouth, the plain gloss she wore made her full lips more kissable. He'd wanted her since high school but his feelings weren't returned. She rebuffed his every advance, and yet he couldn't help himself—he kept trying. She'd had a sweet reputation—was a good student and kind to others. To everyone except him. He grimaced.

Couldn't they put this stupid feud behind them? Wasn't nearly 150 years long enough? The men who had caused it were long in their graves, as were their sons and the sons who came after them. It was time to let it go.

Maybe he could talk to Lennie about it. They could be friends, at least. He wanted more than that, of course. He'd always wanted more than friendship with her. But being friends was a start. Now if he could only get his hands on her cell number. That might take some work.

THE NEXT AFTERNOON, Dylan parked his truck in front of his family's grand historic ranch house and headed inside. He'd spent the better part of his day while he was checking on the herds contacting friends and friends of friends, and had come up with the Lennie's number. Though homes and ranches were far-flung, people in the surrounding areas were actually a close-knit community. Now he wished he knew how to call Lennie without her getting mad. The woman had proven herself to be a hard nut to crack.

That evening, his parents came to the big house for dinner. As everyone dug into the wonderful meal Annie had prepared, his mother asked, "When do you start your teaching job?"

He cleared his mouth with a swallow of sweet tea. "Kids don't go back to school until the first week of September, but teachers start back the third week of August."

His mom searched his face. "You nervous?"

Being a first-year teacher, all sorts of things could go wrong. "Maybe a little though Andy gave me such an in-depth run-through those two days I spent with him in May I feel like I have a handle on things." Andy, the Ag teacher who had been teaching at the high school for 30 years, had just retired and was moving to San Antonio to be close to his youngest grand-kids.

"I'm so glad you got the job, honey." Squeezing Dylan's hand, her blue eyes were full of love and a mother's pride.

He laughed. "They hired me in self-defense since I started bugging Andy and Dave for the job my senior year in high school." After he started college, he sent his old Ag teacher and Dave, his principal, a copy of his grades each semester along with his continuing commitment to fill Andy's job when he retired. "I got good grades, and my Ag professor wrote that letter of recommendation for me, too." He took a drink of tea. "Honestly, I don't know what I would have done if they hadn't given me the job. Working as the local Ag teacher has been my dream for so long that I never planned for anything else."

Taking another bite, he caught his mom's eye and changed the subject. "What do you know about Lennie Duncan?"

His mom raised her brows. "I'm not sure what you mean, son."

Dylan swallowed the food in his mouth. "I'm just saying, I've been away at school for four years. What's going on with her?"

His mom bit back a smile. "I see. Things were pretty rough at the ranch for a few months after her father's stroke. Lennie was still in college. The ranch hands stepped up and, somehow, they managed. Your father offered to help but Evan wouldn't hear of it, of course. Now that Lennie's back home, I hear things are running more smoothly."

Dylan nodded. "Anything else?"

Millie grinned. "She's not seeing anyone as far as I know."

"Oh." Eyes on his plate, Dylan took another bite. That was just what he wanted to hear.

"Why all this interest in Lennie?"

He looked up. "I saw her in the cardiologist's office with her dad."

Millie shook her head. "You could have asked her how she was doing."

"Not with her dad around. Evan would skin me alive."

"Over my dead body," Roy said hotly.

Millie sighed. "This damn feud. I'm so sick of it. The poison it spews on these two families just goes on and on."

Dylan laid his silverware across his empty plate. "My feelings exactly. I wish we could just forget about who took whose land."

"Tell Duncan that. I'd gladly put it behind me," Roy said grimly.

Millie said quietly, "In all fairness, it's his family that feels it was shorted."

"I can't help it that his forebearer was too stupid to pay for the land he wanted, can I?" Roy retorted. "Our ancestor got there first and paid, fair and square."

Millie didn't let it go. "But was it really fair? The Duncan's had already marked it for their own. That's the story, anyway. The 40,000 acres would have made a huge difference in the running of their spread. They were left with only 21,000 acres. When you compare the large size of our ranch, 40,000 disputed acres was a small amount of land for the Govains to haggle over."

Roy pressed his lips into a line. "The Duncans should have gone in to pay for it if they wanted it. It's the way the system worked. They didn't, and we bought it. End of story."

Dylan huffed loudly. "End of story except for 150 years of hard feelings and feud."

Roy scowled. "Evan is a bitter man. He'll never let it go."

Dylan shoved back his chair and stood. "Maybe he won't, but I hope Lennie will. It's time the Duncan/Govain feud ended."

Roy tossed his napkin on the table and made a rude noise. "Good luck with that."

As Dylan strode out of the room, he made a promise to himself. He would make his own luck. He'd find a way to talk to Lennie and hope like hell she welcomed the conversation.

ALSO BY JANALYN KNIGHT

Standalone
Cowboy for a Season
True Blue Texas Cowboy
The Govain Cowboys Series
The Cowboy's Fate
The Cowboy's Choice
The Cowboy's Wish
The Howelton Texas Series
Cowboy Refuge
Cowboy Promise
Cowboy Strong
The Tough Texan Series
Stone One Tough Texan
North Their Tough Texan (October 2020)
Find your next handsome hunk now at:
Janalyn Knight on Amazon[1]

---

1. https://www.amazon.com/Janalyn-Knight/e/
B07RPH8GJ6?ref_=dbs_p_ebk_r00_abau_000000

DEAR READER

THANK YOU SO MUCH FOR reading my books. Drop by janalynknight.com and join my newsletter to be the first to get a look at chapters like this. Or, if you like leaving reviews of the books you read, join my Posse review team at janalynknight.com and get advance copies of my new books in exchange for leaving honest reviews. May all your dreams be of cowboys.

Janalyn Knight

REVIEW

IF YOU ENJOYED THIS book, please leave a review. Reviews are the life's-blood of an author's living and are very much appreciated! Click this link to write a review:

Review on Amazon[1]

---

1. https://www.amazon.com/Cowboys-Choice-Govain-Book-ebook/dp/B07Z4VLWV8/

About the Author

Nobody knows sexy Texas cowboys like Janalyn. From an early age, she competed in rodeo, later working on a ten-thousand-acre cattle ranch, and these experiences lend an authenticity to her characters and stories. Janalyn is an avid supporter of the Brighter Days Horse Refuge and totally owns the title of wine drinker extraordinaire. When she's not writing spicy cowboy romances, she's living her dream—sharing her twenty-acres of Texas Hill Country with her daughters and their families.

Read more at https://janalynknight.com/.

Made in the USA
Las Vegas, NV
28 February 2022